CIRCE'S
MOUNTAIN

CIRCE'S MOUNTAIN

Stories by
Marie Luise Kaschnitz

Translated by Lisel Mueller

Milkweed Editions

Permission to translate and publish the stories in *Circe's Mountain* has been given by the following publishers:

Econ Verlags Gruppe, Claasen Verlag for: *Am Circeo; Eines Mittages, Mitte Juni; Christine.*
Insel Verlag for: *Ferngespräche; Lupinen; Silberne Mandeln; Ein Tamburin, ein Pferd; Der Tag X.*
Scherpe Verlag for : *Das dicke Kind; Der Bergrutsch.*

CIRCE'S MOUNTAIN

© 1990, translation by Lisel Mueller
© 1990, design and graphics by R.W. Scholes

Printed in the United States of America
Published in 1990 by *Milkweed Editions*
Post Office Box 3226
Minneapolis, Minnesota 55403
Books may be ordered from the above address

93 92 91 90   4 3 2 1

ISBN: 0-915943-46-8

Publication of this book is made possible in part by grant support from the Literature Program of the National Endowment for the Arts, the Arts Development Fund of United Arts, the Dayton Hudson Foundation for Dayton's and Target Stores, the First Bank Systems Foundation, the General Mills Foundation, Jerome Foundation, the Star–Tribune/Cowles Media Company, the Minnesota State Arts Board through an appropriation by the Minnesota State Legislature, a McKnight Foundation Award administered by the Minnesota State Arts Board, the Northwest Area Foundation, and the support of generous individuals.

Library of Congress Cataloging-in-Publication Data

Kaschnitz, Marie Luise, 1901-1974.
    Circe's Mountain / stories by Marie Luise Kaschnitz : translated
by Lisel Mueller.
        p.   cm.
    ISBN 0-915943-46-8
    1. Kaschnitz, Marie Luise, 1901-1974—Translations, English.
    I. Title.
    PT2621.A73A26   1990
    833'.912—dc20   90-5432
                                                                     CIP

The paper used in this publication meets the minimum requirements of American National Standard for Information Sciences—Permanence of Paper for Printed Library Materials, ANSI Z39.48-1984.

Translator's Preface

♦

Marie Luise Kaschnitz was born in Karlsruhe, Germany, and grew up in her native country. In 1925 she married the classical archaeologist Guido Kaschnitz von Weinberg, who was affiliated with the German Archaeological Institute in Rome; they had one daughter, Iris Costanza. From the time of their marriage until Guido's death, roughly half of their lives were spent in Rome and the other half in Germany, with frequent travels to countries in southeastern Europe and the Middle East, as well as to ancient archaeological sites on the Italian coast and in Sicily. During World War II and for several years afterwards, they were confined to living in Germany until they were able to resume their residence in Rome. In 1958, two years after Guido's retirement and their return to Frankfurt, he died of a brain tumor. The marriage had been extremely close, and her husband's death was devastating to Marie Luise Kaschnitz, as is evident in the poems, stories, and journals she wrote during the next few years. She continued to live in Frankfurt, and having become famous and much honored, accepted two invitations for lecture and reading tours abroad, one to Brazil and one to the United States during the sixties. She died in Rome in 1974.

She was an enormously prolific and versatile writer, a true woman of letters. Her genres include fiction, poetry, radio plays, a biography of the painter Courbet, literary criticism, personal essays, travel writings and several wonderful "diaries" or "journals." I am using quotation marks because the work does not really fit with our usual definitions of the genre. The books consist of a number of long sections that take off from something heard, seen or otherwise experienced and then go far afield, become stories or essays, or both, with only a tenuous (though never forgotten) connection to the original observation, somewhat like the title story of this collection, which purports to be a series of diary entries.

Though Kaschnitz began publishing poetry and fiction in her twenties and had two novels in print by the time she was thirty-six, all her significant work came late in life. The catastrophe of World War II and its aftermath, the horror, shame and intense suffering, engaged her deeply. Her work of that time, predominantly poetry, reflects that engagement. In her role of poet she thought of herself as both conscience and healer. Altogether she published eight volumes of poetry. Her stories, not counting a few early ones, appeared in three volumes between 1952 and 1966; there are fifty-four of them. They are *tales* in the old sense, stories set around a central event, and most of them are quite brief. As a poet and as an admirer of Ernest Hemingway and Samuel Beckett, Kaschnitz did not care for excess in prose; her language is precise and economical. Every word or phrase is carefully chosen to help elucidate the situation and character. Though the stories are brief, her sympathy and subject matter range widely, owing to her unflagging engagement with the world and to what she calls her "curiosity."

To introduce her fiction to American readers, I have chosen twelve stories that seem to me particularly memorable and reflect her versatility. Italy, her second home, is represented in the setting of five stories; the rest are set in Germany. Except for two set in World War II, all her stories take place during the fifties and sixties—one, "*X Day*," evokes the atom bomb jitters of the late fifties. Remarkably, none of these stories are dated; if anything, their location in time and place serves to underline the universality of their themes. Kaschnitz is concerned with the interior lives of her characters; she explores—or lets them explore—guilt, grief, transformation, sexuality, the effect of severe emotional trauma, and the connection between the living and the dead. Stylistically, the stories range from those containing virtually no dialogue to one consisting entirely of dialogue. She frequently uses a first-person narrator, and the bonds between husbands and wives are strong, reflecting her period and, of course, her experience in her own marriage. A fascination with the parapsychological or fantastic is evident, as is a sense of fatalism, lending some of the stories a haunting quality.

For the most part, her stories are freely invented, but this collection contains three that have an autobiographical basis. "The Fat Girl" stems from her relationship with her older sister during their childhood. "One Day in the Middle of June" and "Circe's Mountain," which deal with a widow's despair and incipient recovery, were published two years after her husband's death and unquestionably express her own feelings. "Circe's Mountain" is a moving and brilliant exposition of the stubborn stratagems of grief and survivor guilt.

"Only by being truthful can a writer hit the bull's-eye," Kaschnitz wrote in a literary essay. Her wonderfully perceptive and surprising stories invariably tell the truth about human behavior.

—Lisel Mueller

Circe's Mountain

Translator's Preface

STORIES BY
MARIE LUISE KASCHNITZ

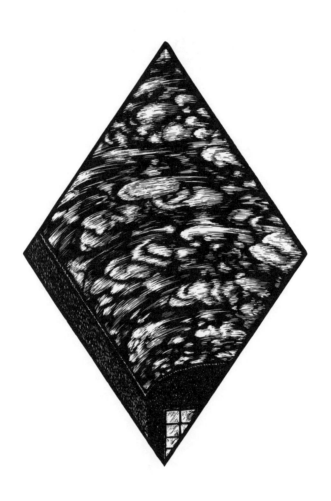

The Landslide

♦

There are those of us who are alive.

There are those of us who are dead and yet alive, like plants, perhaps, or like shells that open a little and let in the sea, or like the colorful algae in the tiny lagoon in the cliff.

Do you remember?

Around seven o'clock in the evening, young Signore Giorgio brought the contract. The contract was written on official paper, which can be bought in tobacco shops and is saturated with the aroma of espresso, cold cigarette ash and the discontent of young men who have been ruined by the tourists.

We walked through the lobby of our hotel with young Signore Giorgio and sat down at one of the small tables which are placed near the open windows. With a graceful gesture young Signore Giorgio removed a fountain pen from his vest pocket and held it out to you. Outside on the terrace, the rods of the awning were clanking in the warm breeze. It had been raining all day; there were puddles on the metal tables, and at the bottom of the steep *macchia* garden lay the evening sea, cobalt blue, like a bowl filled to overflowing.

"Everything is ready," young Signore Giorgio said. "You can move in tomorrow. I'll send Giuseppina down at nine o'clock—ten, if you prefer."

"At nine," I said quickly.

And then we looked at the large, white sheet of paper which listed everything, the rent for the new house and the lease on the tower (a ruin, really), which ran for 99 years, no more, no less. But that was simply a formality and the amount ridiculously low. The house also cost next to nothing because of its remote location, and there really wasn't any reason for us to read the contract again, since we had worded it ourselves and there was nothing left to consider.

Yes, you could have picked up the pen and signed. But you did not, and why not, when we had looked forward to this moment for such a long time—why not? Because at this moment, on the spilling bowl down below, the "Regina Elena" gave her low, pitiful whistle and made all three of us watch her attempts to land, but she couldn't make it into port; she had to steam on with the passengers and the mail, through ink-blue streams and pink reflections of clouds reaching for her like the arms of an octopus.

"You won't have to go hungry tomorrow," young Signore Giorgio said quickly. "My mother will send a fish, mullet, and vinegar and oil."

There was something imploring in the way he looked at us, but he maintained the dignity with which business is transacted in the south: as you wish; you take it, you don't take it; we get the money, we don't get the money. The whites of his beautiful animal eyes were gleaming in the lamplight, but you screwed the top on the fountain pen and handed it back to him and said, "We'll be back after supper, in half an hour, with the signature and the money." The "Regina Elena" sent out one more wail and disappeared behind the promontory; a waiter rang the gong, once, twice, in the lobby, and Giorgio left, swaying rhythmically as he walked.

And then we had supper at a small table among other small tables. Almost all the people were foreigners, people on pleasure trips, birds of passage whose wings would not stop fluttering, straining for flight towards a new destination or towards home. "I'm leaving tomorrow," the Swede at the next table called to us, "I have to get home. I can take you along if you want to come; I have room in my car. I'll be leaving at ten." And at that point you should have said, "No, thank you, we're not leaving; we are staying. We've rented a house. We're going to stay for a year or longer; maybe the rest of our lives." But you only nodded and smiled and said nothing. You did not mention the house and the tower and the 99 years, that magic number, which filled us with delight as well as an

CIRCE'S MOUNTAIN

eerie shudder; nor did you mention the fire signals the Saracens used to send from tower to tower, all along the coastline. You acted as if we were like the rest, ready to take off with our travel tickets in our pockets. And yet everything was different for us, with the official document you were holding, the sweet, heavy scent of spring in the autumn air and the thunder of wagon wheels at the bottom of the cliff wall. And it all belonged to us and we to it; it was like a heavy hand laid on us, which placed us, side by side and close together, in the midst of the flowering *macchia*.

Of course we had wine with our supper; it was part of the meal. It was the red wine of the local hillsides, and our eyes sought each other when we drank it, and you put your arm around me when we walked out into the dark street. And all of this would be no different today, except it would, because the future weighs less than the past, and dreams weigh less than experience, because the unlived life is light, so light.

We walked down the road that runs on top of the cliff, as we did every night, filled with our unlived lives and the robust red wine. We talked about what we would need for the house, the most immediate necessities being cooking pots, bowls and spoons and a spade, so we could dig up the beds underneath the lemon arbor and plant lettuce, firm, green lettuce, to eat for Christmas. And we would order a writing table for you, with a large, sturdy top of olive wood, and when we talked about that, we already heard the saw screaming and splitting the wood, and tasted the young, moist lettuce. As we walked along the road, we saw things, each thing, in a new context, and I remember that for the first time we tried to identify the constellations hanging in the sky and above the mountain ridge. We came to the spot where the landslide had occurred many years ago, and, as always at this spot, we repeated how strange it was that, of all buildings, it should have been the church that was buried and at the precise moment when they were singing the *Te Deum* and ringing the bells, so that the believers must have been dispatched to the sea, to their deaths, in a state of blessedness. Then we had left that place and arrived at the spot where the large bush daisies bloom on the wall, and we decided we would have to have daisies like these, rose-red and white and glowing in the night.

We walked toward the village and through the first long tunnel, and when we emerged from the dusty draft, it was raining again and the sea below the pasta factory was roaring as if it had gone mad. We passed the harbor. There was no one on the waterfront, but inland, on the market square, they were sweeping the pavement, and in front of the tavern there were young men, hats pushed back, hands in their pockets, Giorgio among them, and we could have sat down with him at a table, signed the contract and given him the money, but we did not. We continued along the shore road, past the round tower and around the cliff and through neighboring Atrani, a white fortress in the black rock. And then around the next cliff jutting and past many houses and the small harbor, where the nets are hung to dry next to the fine noodles, which are also drying and which have a golden glow in the lamplight. And then the road started climbing again, and the olive trees on the mountainside were creaking in the west wind; the mountains hung ominously above us; the white heads of foam were tossing, the stars had a watery glitter, and the false scent of spring became purer and more insistent.

Although the moon was not out, it was not really dark, and from a distance we could see the wall and wrought-iron gate that belonged to our house, but we could not see the house itself, which stood farther down among the lemon groves, hidden by the tops of the medlar trees. For a while we stood next to the wall, looking down at the thriving wilderness and across at the tower, which hung black over the glittering waves. We could not resist climbing over the wall and down the narrow, crumbling stairs and reaching for the lemons, unripe but already emitting some fragrance, pure and bittersweet. And then we reached the house, and of course one of the shutters was open so that we could enter without any difficulty. We found a candle, which we lit, and its circle of light illuminated the painted ceiling, and because my hand holding the candle shook a little, it looked as if the small, pink clouds up there were taking off and the funny, big-bellied

CIRCE'S MOUNTAIN

boats were embarking on their voyages. And then I put the candle in a glass and we opened the French entrance doors and stood on the threshold, our shadows huge on the tiles of the terrace, man and wife.

Later we sat down on the bed and talked about what we wanted to buy tomorrow and what we would eat, what we would do the day after tomorrow and the day after that. We kept on talking about the necessary errands, to the boat dock and the post office, about the gardening work and about having a boat built so we could go fishing; then the acetylene lamp of our boat would be among those that line the Bay of Paestum at night like a gleaming wreath. How long we talked I don't know; I know only that every minute rose and set like a full, heavy day. And all the time there was a rushing sound in our ears, from the sea and the trees and the many little rivulets that ran downhill, but it was not raining. Perhaps this was the last day of the equinoctial storms and tomorrow the sun would shine and we would lie in the sun on our cliff, down in the little cove. That's where we were headed now. We had intended to walk to the tower, but the path was too dark and slippery and we couldn't find it. The stairs too were slick and damp. You held my hand and we groped our way step by step, the bushes closing behind us, and though the headlights of the buses on the road above, and the lights of the ships from Africa on the sea below, swept past us, each step took us farther away from any nameable place into a terrifying, nameless country. Because below us in the tiny cove there was only the smell of salt and the flying foam and the roar, a witches' brew of seething froth. And of course we shouted at each other how thrilling it was and looked at each other with laughing faces, but wasn't there something like dread inside us, a sense of foreboding? But that's easy to say, later, when it's all over and everything is known.

Then we climbed up again, two hundred and five steps from sea level to the road, and when we came back to the house, you stepped on the terrace and closed the shutter from the outside. Then I felt as if we were lying on that bed and you closed the door above us like a tomb and I said, "Oh no, don't." But the wind was so strong that when I spoke, I couldn't hear myself. And then we came to the road and for the first time we noticed how steeply the cliff overhung the landscape just at that point. There were strange noises everywhere, gravel being yanked back into the water, olive trees sighing in the wind, wagon wheels whose rolling sounded like thunder in the shadow of the cliff walls. And when we walked through the village and came to the place where we should have turned toward Giorgio's house, you slackened your pace a little, just enough to leave it to me to make the turn, and I didn't do it, I don't know why. I walked straight ahead and then a little later I asked if we hadn't gone past the turnoff and you said, "It's probably too late; they may be asleep." And I thought, "He is afraid to make the decision," and you thought the same about me. But it was something quite different; it was destiny and it lay beyond our will.

Because when we got back to the hotel, the concierge said, "*Che cattivo tempo!*" and handed you the telegram. Not that it was about anything unusual, merely something you had to take care of in Rome. And you thought I should come along and we should accept the offer of the Swedish gentleman. We would be back in a few days. We went cheerfully up to our room, where the bags stood packed, but that night we said nothing more about the house, not a single word. Next morning it had stopped raining. We drove fast down the road we had always walked along, and in the opposite direction, not passing the house. It all seemed strange to me, almost like flight, and around noon I felt a sharp pull, a sense of being pulled away, and I thought that perhaps we existed simultaneously in two places, here in the car, and there in the wild, paradisal garden and the abandoned house beyond the cliffs. And I saw Giorgio's mother walking down with vinegar and oil and fish, and even though she was an old woman, she ran down the steps like a young girl and opened the door and stood there before us in the gold-green light. But of course it isn't true; in reality Giorgio's mother did not walk down those steps to present us with the fish. Because by this time it had already happened.

Yes, it happened around noon, at the time our Swedish

driver pulled off the road near Caserta and we examined our bag lunches. Around that time, due to the effects of the sun's rays, and being subject to mysterious physical laws, a piece of Mount Latteri came loose and began to roll, and coming down it took along everything in its path, medlar trees and pines and lemon arbors and the house with its painted ceiling and its stove and the headfeather fan, and carried it all down to the sea with an enormous rumbling. And all that was left to see was a terrible wound in the flowering body of the earth, a wide bed of destruction that began at the road and continued downward to the bay. And I imagine that in the evening everyone came to look at the wound, and that young Signore Giorgio was there, moving his arms gracefully and telling about the foreigners who are so clever and know everything beforehand, but what good is that to him and his mother; it just means they are worse off than ever.

And at the same time the two foreigners sat in a cafe in Rome and stared at the fat headlines in the *Messagero* and looked at each other, you and I, and our eyes held the question: *saved—for what?* And then we drank and laughed, and we did not return to the coast, not for any particular reason, only because life had other plans for us and wanted us afoot for a long time yet.

Yes, a long time has passed since then, but I can picture it all clearly, and it grows clearer every day. And I know there are those of us who are alive, who have seen many places, known good and bad people, exchanged good and bad words, many words, good and bad, not knowing how it will end.

And there are those of us who were pulled down in a state of blessedness, one noon in October many years ago, and who nevertheless sit in the old house in front of the fireplace and move the headfeather fan back and forth on certain evenings when the reflections of the clouds lie on the ink-blue water like octopus arms.

Who leave the cove in the evening and lure the fish with the harsh lamp of their boat.

Who walk down the cliff road under the damp stars, large, fleeting and eternal, because the unlived life is light, so light.

Long Shadows

Boring, all of it boring, the hotel lobby, the dining room, the beach where her parents lie in the sun, fall asleep with their mouths open, wake up, yawn, go swimming, fifteen minutes in the morning, fifteen minutes in the afternoon, always together. She sees them from behind, her father's legs are too thin, her mother's too fat and with varicose veins; in the water they perk up and splash around childishly. Rosie never goes swimming with her parents; she has to keep an eye on her sisters, who are still little but no longer sweet. In fact, they are silly brats who pour sand over your book or put a jellyfish on your bare back. Having a family is awful, and it's clear to Rosie that other people feel the same way; for example, the dark-skinned man with the gold chain whom she calls the shah. Instead of sitting with his family under the beach umbrella, he hangs around the bar or races the motorboat, wild turns at top speed, always alone. A family is a drag; why can't you be born already grown up, ready to be on your own? "I'm going off on my own," Rosie announces one day after lunch, adding cautiously, "to town, to buy postcards, scenic postcards for my school friends," as if she had any intention of sending cards to those stupid classmates of hers, greetings from the blue Mediterranean, how are you, I am fine. "We're coming too," her little sisters yell, but thank God they can't go, they have to take their afternoon naps. "All right, as long as you take the main road up to the market and come right back," her father says, "and don't talk to anybody," and then he follows her mother and her little sisters, goes off with his thin, hunched office back; he took the boat out this morning but he'll never be a sailor. Up the main road to the town whose

walls and towers you can see glued to the mountain, where
her parents have never yet been, they find the walk too long,
too hot, which it is, no shade anywhere. Rosie doesn't need
shade, why should she; her skin is covered with suntan lotion,
and she feels fine anywhere as long as no one nags at her and
no one asks her questions. When you're alone everything becomes large and strange and starts to belong only to you: my
road, my black, mangy cat, my dead bird, repulsive, riddled
with ants but definitely worth touching, mine. My long legs in
faded linen slacks, my white sandals, one foot in front of the
other, nobody on the road, the sun burning. When the road
reaches the hill, it begins to wind, a blue snake among gold
vine leaves, and the crickets chirp madly in the fields. Rosie
takes the shortcut through the gardens. An old woman walks
toward her, a mummy, unbelievable, the creatures you see
running around when they clearly belong in the grave. A
young man passes Rosie and stops, and Rosie's face becomes
stern. The young men here are obnoxious bums, you don't
need parents to tell you that, what do you need parents for
anyway, they warn you against dangers that are already obso-
lete. "No, thank you," Rosie says politely, "I don't need company," and walks past the young man the way she has seen
the local girls walk, straight back, stiff spine, chin pulled in,
eyes lowered and hostile, and he contents himself with a few
flattering murmurs, which sound utterly inane to Rosie. Vineyards, cascades of pink geraniums, nut trees, acacias, vegetable
beds, white houses, pink houses, her palms sweaty, her face
perspiring. Finally she has reached the top and the town. Rosie
the clipper ship catches the wind and sails happily through
shady streets, past fruit stands and flat tin boxes filled with
colorful, glistening, round-eyed fish. My market, my town, my
shop with its flock of rubber animals and its galaxy of straw
hats, and even its stands of scenic postcards, with Rosie choos-
ing three garishly blue ocean views, just to go through the motions. On the walk, the square, no mental ahing and ohing
over the castle and the church facades, but plenty of other
things to look at, the modest window displays, the ground
floor bedrooms where sentimental madonnas hang above dou-

ble beds with ornate cast-iron bedsteads. There's hardly anyone out at this time of the afternoon; a scruffy little mutt barks at a boy who stands at a window and makes faces at it. Rosie discovers half a roll in her pocket, left over from breakfast. "Catch, pooch," she says and holds it out to the dog, and it dances around her like a trained monkey. Rosie throws out the roll and immediately retrieves it, the ugly little creature hopping on its hind legs makes her laugh; finally she sits on the curb and scratches its dirty-white belly. "Ehi," the boy calls, and Rosie calls back, "Ehi"; their voices echo, and for a moment they seem to be the only two persons awake in this hot, dozing town. When she walks on and the dog follows her the girl is pleased to have company with no questions to answer, to be able to say, come my doggie, now we're walking through the town gate. The gate is not the same one through which Rosie entered the town, and the road does not run down to the beach but uphill; it crosses an oak forest and then, giving full view of the sea, runs along the edge of the fertile slope. Rosie's parents had planned a joint hike up here and on to the lighthouse; how comforting to know that at this moment they are napping in their darkened room at the foot of the mountain. Rosie is in another country, my olive grove, my orange tree, my ocean, my little dog, come bring the rock back. The dog retrieves and barks on the dark blue, melting asphalt strip; now it runs back towards town a little way. Someone is coming around the bend—it's a boy, the boy who was standing at the window making faces, a sturdy, deeply-tanned kid. "Your dog?" Rosie asks, and the boy nods, comes closer and starts to explain the scenery to her. Rosie, who knows a little Italian from a stay in Tessin, is pleased at first, then disappointed; she had already figured out that the sea was the sea, the mountain the mountain and the islands the islands. She walks faster, but the stocky boy sticks close to her and goes on talking; everything he points to with his short, brown fingers loses its magic; what's left is a picture postcard like the ones Rosie bought, dayglow blue and poison green. If only he'd go home, she thinks, he and his dog; suddenly she is tired of the dog, too. When she sees, ahead of her, a trail branching off to the left, leading steeply downhill between the *macchia* and the cliff, she stops, pulls out the few coins she has left from her purchase, thanks the boy and sends him back, forgetting him immediately and enjoying this adventure, this cliff trail, which at times gets lost in the thick brush. Rosie has forgotten her parents and sisters, she has even forgotten herself as a person with a name and age, Rosie Walter, 9th grade, who could do better in school; none of all that, a free-floating soul and in her own defiant way in love with the sun, the salt air, her freedom, an adult like the shah, who unfortunately doesn't take walks, otherwise it would be possible to meet him here and watch for ships passing in the distance, without any inane yakking. The trail becomes a stairway that winds around the cliff. Rosie sits down on one step, explores the fissured rock with all ten of her fingers, sniffs the mint, which she crumbles between her palms. The sun burns, the sea flashes and dazzles. Pan is sitting on the broom-covered hill, but Rosie's education is sketchy, she knows nothing about him. Pan is stalking the nymph, but Rosie sees only the boy, the twelve-year old, Jesus, here he is again; she is extremely irritated. He comes leaping down the mountain stairs on soundless, dusty-gray feet, this time without his dog.

"What do you want," Rosie says, "go home," and is about to continue on the trail, which, at this point, runs alongside the cliff without a railing, with a sheer drop-off to the sea. The boy does not repeat his "Ecco il mare, ecco l'isola," but he won't go home, either; he follows her and makes a strange, almost imploring sound, a sound that isn't quite human and frightens Rosie. What is it, what does he want, she thinks, she wasn't born yesterday, but surely that can't be it, he can't be more than twelve, a child. But it's possible the boy has picked up things from his older friends, his big brothers; there's talk in the town, everlasting low-voiced talk about the foreign girls, so hungry for love and so willing, who walk alone through the vineyards and olive groves, no husband or brother pulls out a gun, and the magic word *amore, amore* brings on their tears, their kisses. Autumn talk, winter talk in the cold, sad café or on the wet, gray, desolate beach, talk that rekindles the heat of summer. Just wait, kid, in two or three years there'll be one for you, she will walk across the square, you will be at the window, and she will smile at you. Then you run after her, don't be shy, kid, what do you mean she doesn't want to, she's just pretending, she wants to.

Not that the boy, the master of the simian dog, remembers such advice at this moment, remembers the great love song, summer song of winter; nor have two or three years gone by. He is still Peppino, the little snotnose who gets smacked when his mother catches him snitching jam from the jar. He can't assert himself like the older ones, swagger and call out, "ah bella" now that he is trying his luck with this girl, the first one who smiled at him and enticed his dog. His luck, he doesn't know what that is, grown-up talk and innuendoes, or does he suddenly know it after all when Rosie steps back, pushes his hand away and, white-faced, flattens against the cliff? He knows, and because he can't make demands, he starts to beg and wheedle in the language foreigners understand, which consists entirely of simple forms, *come please, embrace please, kiss please, love please*, all this thrust out rapidly in a trembling voice, with saliva running from his mouth. When Rosie laughs apprehensively and says, "Come on, what's the idea, how old are you anyway," he steps back but at the same time steps out of his childhood in front of her eyes, knits his brows and looks at her with wild, greedy eyes. I will not let him touch me, I will not let him hurt me, Rosie thinks and looks around for help, but the high road lies beyond the cliff, no one is visible on the zigzag path at her feet, and down at sea level any scream would undoubtedly be drowned out by the surf. At sea level, that's where her parents are about to go for their second swim, where can Rosie be, she was only going to buy some postcards for her school friends. Oh, the classroom, so dark and cozy in November, what a nice painting, Rosie, that bird's wing, we're going to frame it, it deserves to be exhibited. Rosie Walter, with a cross behind her, your dear classmate who died by the blue Mediterranean, never mind how. Ridiculous, Rosie thinks and tries once more, clumsily, to reason with the boy, but at this point greater fluency wouldn't have helped anymore, either. Young Pan, imploring, stammering, burning, must have his nymph; he tears off his shirt and pants and suddenly stands there naked against the yellow bush on a scorching bed of rocks, frightened and silent, and suddenly everything is very still, except for the sound of the garrulous, indifferent sea below.

Rosie stares at the naked boy and forgets her fear, so beautiful does he suddenly seem to her with his brown body, the belt of white skin left by his bathing suit, the crown of yellow flowers around his damp, black hair. But now, he steps out of his golden halo and advances on her with his long white teeth bared; now he is the wolf in the fairy tale, a wild beast. Against animals you can defend yourself; Rosie's own narrow-chested father once proved that; she was quite young then and had forgotten about it, but now it comes back to her. No, no rocks, Rosie, with dogs you have to stare at them hard; O.K., let it come closer, don't blink, see, it's trembling, it's crouching, it's running away. The boy is a roaming dog, he stinks, he's a carrion-eater, perhaps he is rabid, stand very still now; father, I can do it. Rosie, who cowers against the side of the cliff like a bundle of misery, straightens, grows tall, grows up from her child's shoulders and stares at the boy's eyes angrily and fixedly for many seconds without once blinking or moving a muscle. It is still, immensely silent, and suddenly there is an overwhelming fragrance, sweet as honey and bitter as herbs, from millions of inconspicuous shrubs, and in that scent and silence the boy does, really, collapse like a doll whose sawdust is leaking out. What happened is incomprehensible; we only know that Rosie's gaze must have been terrifying, that it must have contained something of a primal force, the primal force of resistance, just as the boy's imploring and stammering, and his last wild gesture, contained the primal force of desire. Everything new, everything experienced for the first time by these children on this hot, brilliant afternoon, the life instinct, desire and shame, the rite of spring, but without love, only longing and fear. Humiliated, the boy retreats under Rosie's basilisk gaze, step by step, whimpering like a sick baby, and Rosie feels ashamed, too, because of the effect of that gaze, which she will never find the courage to repeat, even in front of a mirror. In the end the dog has reappeared, barking its bold, untroubled bark; the boy has run up the steps soundlessly and now sits on the rock wall buttoning his shirt and mumbling something, angry and blind with tears. Rosie runs down the zigzag trail and wants to feel good about having got away, you've got to hand it to fathers, they're good for something after all, but deep down she only feels sad as she stumbles among wolf's-milk and white thornbushes, blind with tears. Your classmate says, Rosie, I hear you were in Italy; yes, thank you, it was beautiful. Beautiful and terrifying, that's what it was, and Rosie washes her face and neck with sea water when she arrives at the shore and thinks, I'm not going to tell, not a word, and then she strolls along the edge of the water towards the bathing beach and her parents, while on the road above, the boy is slowly trotting home. And so much time has passed that the sun is slanting across the mountain and both Rosie and the boy are casting long shadows as they walk, long, widely separated shadows, over the tops of young piñons on the slope, and over the sea, which is paler now.

One Day In The Middle of June

◆

I was just returning from a trip and had no idea what had happened. I went from the train station directly to my apartment building and rang the bell of the lady who had kept my key for me. She greeted me cordially and gave me a meaningful look. "Are you aware that you are supposed to be dead?" she asked. I am not attached to life, but those words of hers bothered me. "Dead?" I asked. "What do you mean?" "Yes," my neighbor said—her name is Mrs. Teichmann—"but you mustn't worry about it; a false death report means you're going to live a long time." I gave a rather forced smile and took the key, which she had kept in a desk drawer. "Who reported my death?" I asked. "A strange woman," Mrs. Teichmann said. "No one knew her; she walked into the building, rang all the bells and told everyone you were dead. She had dark skin and a thin face. I'm sure she was a foreigner."

"An Italian?" I asked.

Mrs. Teichmann didn't know. She remembered that the stranger had carried a magazine; perhaps she went into other buildings to sell subscriptions, but she didn't recall the title of the magazine. There are so many solicitors, male and female; only yesterday a young man came to her door and said only, "Christ is here." And then she reported that the stranger demanded that she hand over my apartment key, right then and there.

"What unmitigated gall," I said, incensed. I thanked her, went into my apartment, unpacked and looked through the heap of second-class mail, which had not been forwarded to me. I tried to forget about the bizarre incident, but I couldn't do it. Coming home from a trip you tend to feel lost, anyway, especially if you are not used to being alone. Things receive you differently from people; at most they ask to be dusted, but they make up for this modesty by flooding you with all sorts of memories. You move around doing this and that—it hasn't always been this silent here—and then you sit down and close your eyes because there is nothing you can look at without hurting. So I sat down and closed my eyes and immediately thought of the strange woman and that it would be good to know more about her, know every last detail.

It was five o'clock and I would have liked to make some tea, but I went to call on the lady who lived below me, Mrs. Hoesslin, and then on the family above me. I found out a few things but not much, and when I was back in my apartment I tried to imagine what it was like that day in the middle of June, around noon. That was two months ago. Hot that month and time of the day; all the women on the stairs, summoned by a loud, foreign voice; Mr. Frohwein, who is a sales representative, about to leave, and the con artist on one of the stairs, acting very sure of herself, almost challenging. "Believe me," she says, "Mrs. Kaschnitz is dead, as sure as I'm standing here." The women shake their heads and Mr. Frohwein involuntarily removes his hat. They are all stunned but not entirely convinced. Since we've lived in this apartment building for a long time, everyone knows me pretty well. Among the residents are people with whom we sat in the basement and flattened ourselves on the floor when the bombs came close. Mrs. Hoesslin had forwarded my mail and I had thanked her on occasional picture postcards showing Roman fountains and the Cape of Circe. One of these, a postcard from the Cape of Circe, had arrived a few days before. I had written that I was fine and my daughter had added a greeting. Thus my death was unlikely, though of course not impossible. There are storms and undertows and sharks; there are accidents and heart attacks, not to mention all the people who choose to leave this world. Reason enough, in other words, to shake one's head thoughtfully, but not reason enough to hand over the keys to a complete stranger.

"As sure as I'm standing here," Mrs. Teichmann says, "that sounds impressive, but who are you? We don't know you; we've never seen you before."

"My name is not important," the woman says quickly. "I have the authority, that's all that matters."

"And why you?" Mrs. Teichmann counters.

The stranger tosses back her hair. "Because," she says, "Mrs. Kaschnitz was all alone in the world, because she had nobody left." Now the women come alive and begin talking all at once. Nobody left, that's not true, that's ridiculous. She had visitors almost every day, friends and relatives; her phone was always ringing, her mail box filled to overflowing. They say all this with great determination and it's surprising that the strange woman hasn't given up by now. She is still on the stairs, standing very erect and calling out loudly, "It's not true, I know better; she had no one, she was all alone in the world."

I had come this far in my reconstruction of the scene, and although this was not quite the end of the story, I got stuck on that last sentence. I couldn't get it out of my mind, and in order to get rid of it I walked around my apartment between the east room and the west room and looked out of the windows. There was a policeman on the street holding a little girl by the hand, and I thought, under such circumstances the police should be notified and it's hard to understand why this wasn't done. Or did they call the police? No, they didn't; Mr. Teichmann merely murmured something to his wife about the police, and in reaction, or perhaps not in reaction at all, the strange woman put the magazine back in her briefcase and left, but not hurriedly. She walked down the stairs very slowly, like an offended queen, without speaking to anyone.

"I must find the woman," I thought. People who sell magazines are on the street or in apartment lobbies and she might be in our neighborhood again. I put on my gloves; I didn't need a jacket because it was still hot, an endless summer. I walked down the street and waited in or outside of various buildings, and then I followed the same procedure in neighboring streets, even inquiring in the shops about the stranger. But no one had seen her, then or now, and the only vendors left on the street were a scissors grinder and a man with an apple cart, but he had already covered up the apples and was going home. It was about to get dark; days were getting shorter and nights longer; even the hottest summer can't conceal that change. On my way home I was going to stop at the precinct police station, but it had been moved and I was suddenly very tired and did not feel like going elsewhere. I also thought of the bother the police would be for the residents in my building; they might even be made to feel guilty. They would be questioned and no doubt give contradictory evidence. Was the woman wearing a hat, yes, no, of course not, or did she, maybe, and in the end they would look like criminals, even though they acted with common sense and didn't hand over the key. Obviously they didn't want to get involved with the police or they would have called them earlier; this person had been too scary, someone who might have returned to take revenge, like placing a bundle of packing jute on the basement stairs and setting it on fire. It would have been child's play since, unfortunately, the door to our building was always open.

So I did not go to the police station; I went home, and at home I thought of something and took out my small notebook, a calendar, really, with lots of room for writing beside the dates. It had suddenly become extremely important to know what had happened to me on that day in the middle of June, though I couldn't have said why.

Friday the thirteenth, Saturday the fourteenth, Sunday the fifteenth of June. I didn't know the exact date on which the stranger appeared. To ask my neighbors to try and remember that would have been asking too much. Around noon in the middle of June, they all agreed on that; this eliminated Friday because Mrs. Hoesslin was in the Taunus Mountains, also Saturday because Mr. Frohwein did not drive off on his rounds then, and Sunday because no one peddles magazines on Sunday. On Mondays the woman above me has her cleaning woman in, who surely would have been curious enough to step into the stairwell also. This left only the seventeenth or the eighteenth. I searched for the two dates in my calendar, but not hastily, standing next to my two partially unpacked suitcases. Quite formally I sat down at my desk, after closing the curtains and turning on the floor lamp, as if I were about to make God knows what discovery. Nothing was written down for the eighteenth, and for the seventeenth very little, only the words "drink," "drown," and "Orfeo," which I did not understand.

I have often wondered why we dare to write down certain things only in an arcane code, things which we may later reveal quite freely but which at the time have not yet been transformed, are still dangerous. I thought of this now: dangerous, danger, the danger flag, a little piece of red fluttering from the bamboo pole on the beach. A storm, an undertow, danger, don't go in the water. But no, that's not how it was that day around noon in the middle of June; I suddenly remembered it exactly. A deep blue sky, the familiar mirror of the sea lapping at the beach in tiny waves, a scalding sun, the sand burning. The hour of Pan, the relentlessness of the south, and me swimming out to sea, by coincidence all alone. My black clothes, black stockings, black shoes, are lying on the sand under the beach umbrella. Costanza and her girlfriend and Mango and the engineer have gone to get something cold to drink; the bar is a few steps up and faces away from the sea; the juke box next to the dance floor roars and sobs and falls silent. The English children are being called to lunch; whoever is left on the beach blinks into the sun and remains motionless. The water along this coast is very shallow; by the time I can swim I am far from shore and can no longer make out the faces and figures. I lie on my back, borne by the heavy salt water; I needn't move a muscle and my hands are clasped behind my head. The houses are very small; above them rise the woods, and, still higher, the cliffs, the head of Circe bent back in a gesture of pain and turned to stone. You no-good sorceress, I think, you miserable failure, you could not hold Odysseus in spite of all your arts; if someone wants to leave, he will leave even if you promise you will love him forever; if he has to wander, he will wander, and if he has to die, he will die. Then I stop thinking, swim on, keep my eyes open under water and look at the pattern the waves have made deep down in the fine sand. To come up out of the water is terrifying, unspeakably lonely; I should swim back, get dressed, have lunch. But why bother, everything is over, I couldn't hold you, Odysseus, you moved on to fulfill your destiny, on to Ithaca, and Ithaca is death. I am no sorceress, no immortal, I will not turn to stone and pit myself against the sky as a grisly monument. I can drink, drown, sink down into the deep and climb the heights, above and below are the same, above and below are the blessed spirits, you are above and below. An accident, a heart attack; no one needs to feel guilty. To drink, to drown, and the water is already foaming, more agitated, a grayish-white, greenish-white whirlpool presses against my chest. Deeper, a little deeper, now it crushes my chest, chokes off my breath, but where does that sound come from, the sound of a flute; Costanza does not take her flute to the beach, the sand would ruin it and anyway I couldn't hear her play this far from shore. But I do hear it, the voice of a flute that has nothing to do with rococo or pastoral music but has a wholly new tone, strong and wild. And no, I'm not thinking—as far as one can think in seconds—I'm not thinking Costanza is still alive, life is not meaningless, I am not all alone in the world. Because I know children are children, they move into their future; you can enjoy them and get annoyed at them and worry about them, but they cannot help you. And yet it's this mysterious flute, this call from life, which pulls me up out of the water coughing and sputtering, which impels me to lie on my back to rest and begin moving my arms shoreward. And on the beach there is Costanza waiting with the beach towel and saying angrily, "What possessed you to swim out so far, don't you know there are sharks out there?" We gather up our things and I say, "Don't forget your flute," and she looks at me blankly. It was twenty minutes past twelve; at that time the strange woman had already left our building—why, surely not because she was afraid of the police?

CIRCE'S MOUNTAIN

That was something I had to find out yet, and I got up from my desk blind-eyed and stiff-legged and went to see my neighbor, who had already gone to bed and merely opened up a tiny window in her door.

"Excuse me," I said through the little window, "I didn't understand why the woman who said I was dead finally left, and I'd really like to know that."

"Are you still thinking about that," my neighbor said. "I told you a false death report means a long life."

"Yes, but I'd still like to know," I said.

"Didn't I tell you?" Mrs. Teichmann asked amiably. "Someone mentioned your daughter. That's when she gave up and disappeared."

Mrs. Teichmann shivered and yawned; it was almost eleven.

"Did you report it to the police?" she asked.

But I had not gone to the police and I had no intention of going.

Silver Almonds

◆

The schedule for the day of celebration had been set up weeks ago, down to its last detail. Mass, with a special blessing for the silver wedding couple; then a reception at home, where the gifts would be displayed and vermouth and cookies served, and then, with everyone assembled, the departure for the Campagna, towards the mountains. Lunch in Albano; people who marry young are still youthful on their silver anniversary; they don't have gray hair and don't have to watch their eating and drinking because of narrowing blood vessels. So the menu will start with spaghetti *alla Bolognese*, although that will be preceded by an antipasto of spicy red sausage, olives, and salted salmon. Then *pollo alla cacciatore,* veal in a caper sauce, and finally *zuppa inglese,* that wet sponge of rum-soaked cake, accompanied by coffee and silver-glazed almonds. And let's not forget the wine: several golden Castelli wines, sweet wines and Asti Spumante. The coffee will wipe out the bad effects of the wine, and vice versa. After lunch, which is bound to take up several hours, they will all drive around the lake on the new tourist road and get out somewhere for a walk, provided the weather is pleasant, and why wouldn't it be in the beautiful month of May. A short walk in the woods, tossing a few balls back and forth with the kids; they'll have a radio along, in fact, Mauro, one of the men, has a tiny Japanese one that he carries in his pants pocket and scares people with: a ventriloquist, a walking song.

After the walk it will be too hot or too cool; at any rate they will stop in a cafe in Marino, or perhaps in Castelgandolfo, the Pope's summer residence, where the last event of the day will take place, the most important one for Concetta.

And precisely because it is so important, she has not put it into the program and does not talk about it. She has discussed it only with her confessor, and her confessor made a telephone call and said, yes, it could be done, only she would have to be sure to be on time—and why not, it's a long day.

Ordering the menu and consulting with her confessor about that certain matter is not the extent of Concetta's preparations for her silver anniversary. All the presents she has received during her lifetime, the silver-plated vase, the gold chains and bracelets, which have been pawned and redeemed many times, must be brilliantly polished; the wax flowers, tulips and daffodils, have to be dusted, the tiles scrubbed with sulphur water. The hand-embroidered tablecloth and its matching napkins have been freshly washed and are fluttering on the roof terrace. Concetta does not intend to wear her own jewelry on this special day; if she did, there would not be enough left on the gift table for her friends and relatives to admire. A silver wedding is not like the first wedding: it is a demonstration of your value, what you are worth to others and thus to yourself. And so, as soon as she hangs up the table-cloth and napkins, Concetta starts on her rounds, traveling by *circulare*, by bus, on foot, and on the streetcar again. All the ladies Concetta used to work for, cleaning or doing the washing, happen to be at home: *Concetta, how wonderful to see you, and a silver wedding!* And they note down the date in green and red purse-sized calendars. Concetta invites them to the church and the reception, mentally calculating the presents she can expect; she asks after their children, their brothers, their sisters; she's in no hurry to leave. She knows the jewelry boxes of the ladies, some of them leather with velvet interiors, others soap containers padded with pink cotton. Would it be possible to borrow a piece of jewelry just for her silver wedding day, say the gold chain with the little madonna on it, say the ring in the shape of a snake with ruby eyes, say the filigree bracelet? The ladies are friendly, they don't mind a bit, why should they. *Goodbye, Concetta, best wishes, Concetta,* and Concetta, who has put the carefully tissue-wrapped pieces of jewelry into her deep handbag, walks rapidly down the stairs and towards the nearest public conveyance. When she gets downtown she stops off at the sweet shop that specializes in wedding almonds. The charming little containers in which the candied almonds are handed out to the guests are also furnished. Concetta has to choose, and she is in despair because she falls in love with the kind that's decorated with little dolls in rococo dress, but she is sensible, and in the end she settles for a modestly priced style of heavy glass. After all, they are poor people; the print shop where her husband works doesn't pay much; only since Paolino, their 17-year-old son, has been earning money, have they been better off. Since then they have been able to exchange their single room for an apartment, although except for the bed, the wardrobe and the television cabinet, it's practically empty, so that they'll have to borrow some furniture for the celebration. After the sweet shop Concetta heads for home, where the seamstress is waiting for her on the stairs, not a real seamstress, of course, but a friend who knows how to sew. The dark amber silk is a present from Concetta's last employer, who for that reason—delicacy on Concetta's part—has been eliminated from the list of jewelry lenders. "Bice, come in," Concetta says, "I'm dead, I'm suffocating," and she pulls her shoes from her swollen feet and her girdle from her hips and drinks a glass of water. "It's so hot already, what's it going to be like by next Thursday? Bice, I've got to show you the big present." Concetta has bought the big present herself; it's in the wardrobe behind Franco's socks. Concetta puts it around her naked, sweaty shoulders for a moment; she is in her slip, ready to try on the silk. The narrow marten pelts shine in the evening sun, which falls through the window onto the mirror, and Concetta's wet fingers stroke the golden fur, which smells like a zoo. "Maybe it won't get all that hot; we could get thunderstorms or rain; once we even had snow in May." "That's all we need," Bice says, with her mouth full of pins, and Concetta sighs and takes off the fur piece with its stitched-together little heads. There's no way of predicting the weather; weather is made by God.

God makes the weather, and on the silver wedding day he brews up a fine sirocco, a bowl of haze and quivering heat,

but that's not apparent in the morning; in the morning everything is all right. The guests are picked up at nine, and the
pickup is preceded by lengthy discussion: three taxis with
eight passengers each, that's against police regulations, but the
penalty is less than an extra taxi would cost. Besides, they
might not meet up with any police, and even if they should,
the police might look the other way. In church the Ave Maria
is played; Concetta and Franco are in front, kneeling, Franco
in his good blue suit and Concetta in her light brown dress
and matching jacket; the little fur heads lie on her back and
the pelts fall down in front like the braids she wore as a girl.
Then the organ plays the march from *Lohengrin* and the priest
addresses the couple in a low, intense voice. Concetta listens
politely but with some impatience; she worries about things at
home, whether the iceman has been there and whether her
14-year-old daughter Nanda might have one of her headaches.
"This is a beautiful ceremony," she thinks, "but I know something even more beautiful, a surprise for everyone, who else
has that, who else can do that, it was my idea, mine." At
home the gift table is ready and excites admiration; the flowers
are placed in water. "White lilacs, two-thousand lire," Concetta thinks, "eleven red roses, fifteen-hundred, a bunch of
calendulas, pretty shabby." The sky has clouded up and it's
getting muggy. The guests are drinking vermouth-and-seltzer;
Concetta and Franco join them and clink glasses with everyone. Son Paolino is a young man and not too happy about all
the kissing; daughter Nanda hands out the silver almonds in
their glass cases; Concetta's brothers' faces turn red and their
voices grow loud. At eleven-thirty the taxis drive up again; all
three have their radios tuned to the same music, currently
popular songs from a festival in Nice, which inspire the guests
to sing along so loudly that Concetta's ears hurt. The ride is
enhanced by the fact that the guests ask the taxi drivers to
race each other on the road leading out of town, in the thick
of traffic. They stop twice to drink wine in country cafés
along the way. They drive along the Via Appia; jasmine is in
bloom behind all the garden walls. During the stops there's
lots of picture-taking: the wedding couple alone, with their

CIRCE'S MOUNTAIN

children, with relatives, and Concetta makes sure all her jewelry shows, the golden snake, the coral earrings, the filigree bracelet.

Lunch in Albano takes almost three hours. Paolino gives an embarrassed speech in honor of his parents, Nanda giggles, Concetta's brothers have exchanged their wives and are blowing wine-damp kisses into their ears. "If you knew," Concetta thinks between the veal and the dessert, "if you knew what is coming," and she drinks a little less than the others, though she samples all the food and her body expands. She can't remove her girdle here, only strip off her patent leather shoes discreetly under the table. Around four she has everyone get set for the walk, and walk they do, high above the spooky eye of the lake. The little nieces and nephews are supposed to play ball, but they don't want to. It takes a herd of sheep to rouse them from their post-lunch lethargy; they run after the sheep and disappear. The men sit down on a large, flat rock and play cards; the birds sing like crazy in the new chestnut leaves. Concetta has to run after the children in her high heels; Nanda has a headache by now and makes cold compresses with water from the creek; the rest are horsing around. Concetta runs and runs, the little marten paws knock against her chest. "Let them go," her sister-in-law calls, "we aren't in any hurry!" But Concetta knows what they might miss. She runs and calls, "Come on, little darlings!" And the little darlings, dirty and out of breath, finally trot back to the taxis with her. "What heat, what thirst," the grownups say as they get in again. Concetta too has a dry throat and wet spots under her arms. Now it's time to count the calls of the cuckoo: O, it is calling over and over, endless life, endless happiness. In Marino they stop again and drink wine, and the wine finally goes to Concetta's head. She rises and staggers; they all tease her. She sits down again and knows nothing, not how she got to this long table underneath the trees, why she is singing now and beating out the rhythm with her snake-ringed hand, or why the lake rises in front of her eyes and then falls back, up and down, while the children throw silver almonds across the table. Concetta has the feeling there is something she should be doing, something urgent, but she can't remember; she is suddenly very tired and plays with her braids. Franco, whom she knew as a boy, once pulled them tight around her throat: "Watch out, I'm going to strangle you." *It was spring then, too, and the cuckoo was calling, but my braids have claws, sharp little claws, and I'm sick, I've got to throw up, get up Concetta, go inside.* She does not get up and the nausea passes, but now tears are running down her cheeks because she remembers what she has still planned for this day, the real event, the surprise, and she knows now that it will not happen; her feet hang small and limp from her swollen legs and refuse to carry her, and all the others lean across the table with indistinct moon faces. It would have been only a few hundred yards to the Villa; a hundred steps to the balcony from which the Holy Father bestows his blessing today. True, it's meant for foreign pilgrims, but Concetta has received special permission; the Pope would have blessed her and Franco and Paolino and Nanda; with his blessing they would have lived to be a hundred in good health, and Paolino and Nanda would have married and had innumerable sons. But now it is getting dark, too late for admission to the courtyard, and the blessing is over.

"What's wrong, Mammina," asks Nanda, and the sisters-in-law call out, "She's crying, get her some coffee, or would you rather have ice cream?"

"Let's go home," Franco says, and they all rise and squeeze into the taxis, with the weeping Concetta seated between her husband and her sister-in-law, Rosa. She won't stop sobbing, and when the three taxis start to move, she begins screaming. She is having horrifying visions of what is to come: dreadful, tormenting illnesses that will kill her and Franco, Nanda raped, and Paolino crushed on his Vespa by a truck. Her town, destroyed by nuclear war, lies in ashes, the Horsemen of the Apocalypse pictured on her calendar are galloping through the clouds above the debris.

"Hey, pipe down," Franco shouts. He has abandoned the good manners of a bridegroom and feels like a man who has been drinking with other men, superior to all the women in the world. The taxis roll down the Albanian hills; people are hot and scrunched together, they argue and then they stop, their gesticulating hands come to rest, their heads drop on a sweaty shoulder or on their own chests. And so it happens that no one in the party except the drivers, who are stopped at the crossing, notices what passes by behind a cordon of police: two motorcyclists with white helmets, followed by a black limousine with illuminated white silk interior, in which a tired old man, also dressed in white, is riding back to Rome through the dark Campagna and lifting his hand now and then in a gesture of blessing.

Lupines

"We'll risk it," they had said and talked it all over in detail, even drawn a map, during the long evenings, the nights they waited for the bell, or maybe not the bell, maybe just their rifle butts against the door, *Open up, Jewish trash, time to get on the train*. The trains departed from a certain station and covered a certain route; people who knew the city and its environs know the curves, the underpasses, the single-family houses with the enormous bottles painted on their fire walls, the spotty patches of woods with their scraggly brush. There was a place where all trains slowed down; this had been true already when the sisters were children and went to their relatives in the country on weekends to pick currants and gooseberries, and there used to be lupines in bloom along the railroad tracks. One could have jumped off and run alongside the train, and as a matter of fact, Fanny, the older by six years, did just that once, jumping back on the train with an armful of lupines. Of course their parents were not along on this trip. Barbara, the fearful one, had felt her heart in her throat, then and later, each time they rounded the wide curve of the lupine bed. But in the year 1943, when the two sisters waited night after night for the deportation, it was Barbara who had suggested the plan: jump off fifty yards beyond the short tunnel; there are garden plots with wooden sheds; there's an alder grove; there's a hidden trail back to town. And she was the one who yanked the door open and jumped, while Fanny remained seated, lethargic and indifferent, as if there were no such thing as memory; as if she could not escape her destiny, the camp in Poland, the gas chamber, the anonymous death.

This story is about Barbara, who got away, who rolled

down the embankment. There were shouts and a few shots, but nothing more: she would be picked up by the next transport, no point in making the train stop on her account. Barbara hid in the gardens until dark and then simply walked home. According to plan, she would not ring the bell but throw some rocks against the window, and her brother-in-law would not respond immediately but come down after some time to open the door to his sister-in-law Barbara and his wife Fanny. Except that only one returned, the wrong one, as Barbara told herself when she launched the pebbles and saw a shadow move behind the window panes, and when later someone came down the stairs in his sock feet. All this happened more than a year ago, the waiting in the humid west wind, her face buried in the honeysuckle, while her sister rode on and on and their childhood garden with its currants and gooseberries had disappeared long ago. Her brother-in-law had opened the door cautiously and the girl had slipped past him into the building. "Just you," the man had said and Barbara had answered, "Just me." Her brother-in-law had not spoken another word all evening; he sat at the table holding his head in his hands, and he gave no instructions until morning. What he said then had been discussed a hundred times: no going near the windows, no shoes when walking around the apartment, no talk except in a low voice, and if worst came to worst, hide in the storage bin in the attic; be a shadow, a nothing. What was to apply to two now only applied to one, and it was really easier because the two of them would have felt like talking, maybe even like laughing sometimes, and maybe her brother-in-law wouldn't have minded if Fanny had come back alone, maybe that's what he counted on. Fanny alone, slipping into bed with him, and perhaps they would have shed a few tears for their sister and sister-in-law, but everything would have been in order, the awesome order of marriage, which is a bulwark against deception and death. Only it didn't turn out like that, no whispering in the double bed; instead there's Barbara in her little room and across the wall the stony man who surely can't understand why Barbara did not pull her sister from the moving train. But no one can

48
CIRCE'S MOUNTAIN

imagine how quickly such things must be done, and that at such times the scaredy-cat is overcome by reckless determination while the courageous one freezes in her seat.

"I must make him understand," Barbara often told herself during the following months when she was sitting across from her brother-in-law at supper, but she knew he would not be able to understand, neither this nor many other things. He personally was not a target; he was Aryan and blond with gray skin, and a city employee, and it was only his chronically dislocated shoulder that kept him out of the war. A man who lifted his arm twenty times a day at the proper angle for the required salute but listened to a British radio station in the evening, hunched over the murmuring box. Fanny and he, he and Fanny; a separation had been out of the question as far as he was concerned. He thought he could protect her and he wanted to protect Barbara, too, but perhaps when his sister-in-law had come to live with them it became too much, two women in the apartment, two yellow stars coming and going and whispering together in the evening, things he wasn't supposed to hear and didn't want to hear. Now the yellow stars have set; Fanny is God-knows-where and so is Barbara; she does not exist. There is little she can do to help her brother-in-law, cooking for example, because no smell of food must reach the stairwell until after he is home, and no sound of dishwashing once he has left. He often goes out at night now, to a bar or a meeting; in fact, he has joined the Party and the S. A. recently; occasionally he wears a brown uniform. He does these things so as not to attract attention, not to jeopardize Barbara's safety; she knows that. She would like to be nice to him; she is grateful, nothing more, though the thought of something more is hardly far-fetched between two such lonely people, a man and a woman waiting for the same day through the fall and the winter and the spring, and still the day does not come. But Barbara's brother-in-law rejects her gratitude. He does what is expected of him, and Barbara has the feeling that he dislikes her but goes through the motions of behaving correctly: a correct antagonist of the regime, a correct pro-Semite. Barbara looks bad because she never gets outside, and her brother-in-law looks bad because the two of them are living off his one ration card. He can't get things under the table because that would attract attention: what does a widower need a rabbit for, why such a large bag of flour, a whole case of wine. He has been a widower since last Christmas Eve, when the printed announcement reached him, but it became evident then that he had given up his wife as lost a long time ago, on the night Barbara returned without Fanny. As a matter of fact, once the announcement came he began talking to Barbara again, communicating this and that to her in his dry way, but only unpleasant things: the Allies were repulsed in such and such a place, the grocer's Jewish wife had committed suicide. When he returned from Party meetings, where he was forced to join in the singing, and even the swaying back and forth on festive occasions, his mood was especially black. One night he said, "Why am I doing all this? I'm an S. A. member, I have a revolver; I could put one bullet through your head and another through mine. If it wasn't for my mother in Hamburg, I would have done that long ago." Barbara said nothing, but she was trembling; she was twenty years old and had hoped that everything would pass. She had even sat upstairs in the storage bin, a pale-faced sprite, giggling and singing, "Everything passes, everything must end," while watching the clouds drift by. She no longer did this now, but sat in the living room and covered the empty pages of her school notebooks with large suns and moons and little men who walked hand in hand in some sort of zoo or paradise. But eventually she gave up on this, too, even before the first bombs fell.

For a long time the small town, unimportant and away from the main routes, had been spared from air attacks. From listening to illicit military radio broadcasts, the brother-in-law knew the bomb targets by their code names, and also whether the bombers would fly past on the left or the right; he sat over the radio and made gestures not to worry. People didn't yet go down to the cellar, though the one in their apartment building was provided with old chairs, sand and a first-aid cabinet, as the regulations required. On the night the bombs fell on the town the brother-in-law was by the radio again, but

　　　　　　　　　　　CIRCE'S MOUNTAIN

he didn't gesture; he turned out the light, pulled up the black shades and remained at the window, while the first "Christmas trees" came down and the anti-aircraft started up. The apartment building came alive; children were hustled down the stairs, someone knocked at the door and called, "Mr. Kopfinger!" but he didn't move. Barbara couldn't go to the cellar and her brother-in-law didn't go, something Barbara didn't understand, since he was always leaving her alone and left her alone even now, walking from window to window in the dark room and delivering messages of doom. *That was the cement factory; now the school is burning; now they are coming here.* He acted the same way during subsequent attacks and became more and more puzzling to the girl; she didn't know if he hated her or if he was so unhappy that he wanted things to be so bad that they could hardly get worse. One afternoon before he came home she turned on the radio, though she was forbidden to do so, and got a different slant on the news: the Americans had landed in Normandy, an event that the domestic broadcasts couldn't hide and the foreign ones reported on in detail. Good news for all who hated the regime, the tyranny under the sign of the running cross and the double streaks of lightening.

Barbara jumped up, put on a bright dress and reached outside the window surreptitiously to break off some grapevine leaves, which she put on the table in a pitcher. The meal was ready, the thermos filled with the liquid that was officially designated as a "hot drink." Her brother-in-law did not come home at the usual time; it was after midnight when he blundered up the stairs, drunk. Barbara, who had never seen him in such a state, was frightened and retreated into her room. Next morning she did not dare to mention either the landing or the drinking, not even when her brother-in-law, who had noticed the resetting of the radio dial, reproached her severely. "But everything will turn out all right now," Barbara thought helplessly, and she filled the afternoon hours with cutting and brushing her hair, so that by evening she looked like Fanny, whose hair style she had unconsciously adopted. Her brother-in-law came home, stared at her and went to bed immediately. During the next few days he took the trouble of informing her about some of the latest events, but added quickly that things didn't move all that fast. As everyone knows, he was right about that; it took many more months before the war was over. Barbara's patience lasted through the summer; she tried to keep up her brother-in-law's spirits, though he came home drunk more and more often, and one night went into the pantry and ate up their week's ration of bread. In the morning he was sorry, which made his face look even gloomier than usual. Another night he grabbed the girl brutally and arrogantly, as if to say, *you've got to be good for something,* and when she resisted fiercely, he let her go contemptuously: *all this hassle, and not even that.*

Life is full of puzzles. It must have been especially puzzling for young Barbara, who secretly loved her brother-in-law and had hoped some day to take her sister's place, and who could not understand why everything should be different for her, no love, no hope for happiness. One evening in late summer her brother-in-law had torn open her blouse. In the morning the sun was hot and the bushes golden. As soon as she was alone Barbara opened the windows wide and stood in the sun, visible to anyone, and felt the hot sun on her skin. There was no one on the stairs or in the front yard, and when Barbara walked down the slightly downhill street, no one saw her either. It was a quiet morning except for the sound, now and then, of chestnuts bursting and casting their reddish-brown fruits before the girl's feet. Barbara picked up one of them, rubbed it against her cheek and then put it in her pocket to play with. Where to, nowhere, just to be out in the air, her feet pointing the way, feet which, unused to walking, alternately stumbled and danced. Her feet took her out of town; hadn't there been a secret trail with barberry bushes, and didn't one see the railroad tracks when one came out in the open? Barbara saw the tracks, the wide curve around the garden plots; the lupines had stopped blooming, there was only a pear tree, its autumnal foliage pale red and brass yellow. The trail ran towards the tracks; it was the place where all trains slowed down, where twelve years ago, a hundred years ago,

Fanny had jumped off and picked flowers. Barbara stopped and looked around; the unfamiliar sky, the unfamiliar brightness, mixed up her sense of chronology. From a great distance she spotted a train coming from town. A bunch of shabby, rattling wartime cars, not a Jewish cattle car transport but a special train evacuating children, and hundreds of children leaned from the windows. Barbara ran as fast as she could and tried to hoist herself up the embankment by clutching at the faded lupines, but the stalks, with their dry mysterious rattle, came loose from the ground and remained in her hand. For a moment Barbara stood on the embankment gasping in the warm October wind, knowing nothing, wanting nothing, simply allowing herself to fall into the jolting, stomping and rattling of the train. A suicide, they said when Barbara's unrecognizable body was taken to the morgue, and, identified by no one, buried in a pauper's grave. But the few old people who had been in their tiny gardens and watched the incident from among dwarf asters and late roses, testified unanimously that the victim had been a child who had tried to catch the train and had held a bunch of faded lupines in her arm.

A Tambourine, A Horse

♦

A house at the edge of the woods, a single-family dwelling, not
grand, but not poor either: one story topped by two dormer
rooms with slanting walls. A child sleeps in one of those
rooms, and a jumping jack hangs above her bed. It hangs
slackly and has a string between its legs. Before she goes to
sleep, the child pulls on the string; there's still a little light
coming into the room, and the jumping jack pulls up his legs
in the striped pants as high as he can. The child is an eleven-
year-old orphan, contented with her life, who likes school,
likes helping her foster mother around the house and walking
with her foster father along the stretch where the old railroad
man clocks the train, notes down each minute it is late. Most
of the time there's a war going on. Troop transports and pris-
oner transports roll through the birch woods and, on a low
embankment, through bogland. The little town is not close
enough to the border for the inhabitants to be evacuated and
there isn't any shooting, only one day the foreign soldiers ar-
rive and move into everyone's home.

For several days the child has heard her foster parents
whisper anxiously: *we are old and the child is a child, we give
them whatever we have, nothing will happen to us.* The child
doesn't know what it is that might happen to her; soldiers
have food and hand out food; one of them gave her some
candy once. When they start banging on the front door in the
night, the child is scared, but not too scared. "Get dressed,"
her foster father is calling, and right after that, "yes, we are
coming," and already his light step can be heard on the stairs.
A few minutes later they all stand in the entrance hall, the foster parents, the child, and the foreign soldiers who, as it turns

out, are not intent on moving in or on looting but are looking for someone they think is hiding out inside the house. But the child knows there is no one in the house, and when the foster parents shake their heads, she shakes hers. The soldiers' faces turn ugly; one of them grabs the foster father by the shoulder, yanks him around, pokes a gun in his back and forces him to walk ahead of him through all the rooms, including the kitchen and the pantry; finally they walk up the stairs. Next to the child's room is another, equally small, with equally slanting walls, which had at one time been used as a guest room (but there've been no visitors for a long time), then as a food storage room, but now there is not food to store and the room is filled with junk. Just recently the foster mother took the key out of the lock and said, "Put it into the tambourine, child," and the child, who had initially dropped it into her apron pocket, thinks that's what she did, since her foster parents keep their keys in that round little calfskin with its rim of bells, a gypsy instrument from a costume trunk. Now, in the night, they stand in front of the room where someone is supposed to be hiding out; the soldiers rattle the door and the foster father sends the child to fetch the tambourine, which she locates quickly in its customary place in the kitchen cupboard. The child carries it up the stairs as speedily as she can; she senses that the usual tinkling and clattering are not appropriate now and wraps her apron tightly around the bells and the dancing keys. All through the house the light is on, but outside the window by the stairs, gardens, meadows and woodland lie in eerie pre-dawn darkness, and only now does the child feel uneasiness, a faint sense of fear, as if things might turn out badly and never return to what they were. The foster father takes the tambourine from the child; his hands are so shaky that the keys perform a miniature drum roll on the calfskin, a sound that frightens and enrages the soldiers. Suddenly all four of them point their revolvers, and they all speak at once in a language the child does not understand. Finally the only one who knows some German yells, "Open up!" and the foster father is already pulling a key out of the tambourine, but it isn't the right one. The second key he holds out to the soldiers doesn't fit the lock either, neither does the third or fourth. "But it's got to be here," the foster mother says several times in a row and starts to cry. She has forgotten that she gave the child the key to put away, and the child has forgotten it too; she doesn't remember until much later. It's obvious that the soldiers think the whole long, clumsy search is a trick; furious, they rummage around in the tambourine, which by now is almost down to very small keys, the kind that are used for trunks and padlocks. And then the child, who is squatting on the floor picking up the keys the angry soldiers have thrown down, hears two sharp shots and thinks someone is shooting through the window from the no longer familiar, spooky terrain outside. Something falls toward her heavily, a crumpled body which gets stuck among the legs of the soldiers, and a head which keeps slipping down and comes to rest beside the child's hand. It's some time before the child recognizes her foster father's jacket and pink bald head with its corolla of white curls. Her foster mother has fallen on her face; her frail body has been pushed aside by the soldiers, and the child, who has been forgotten, scoots down the stairs on her belly. Later she doesn't remember how she got away from the house, only that in her memory three things blend together: the icy brushing of the high, wet grasses against her calves, the heavy blows with which the soldiers break open the door upstairs, and the ringing of the tambourine, which the child is holding in her hand again without knowing how or why. There is still hardly any light, and in the woods it's even darker, much too dark for a little girl who is running away from something and doesn't know where to go. It would be good to hide, but the child stays on the white, sandy road, running and running without thinking and without any real awareness of what has happened. No sense of grief for the beloved foster parents, no sense of being all alone in the world. Only of cold, cold—and wasn't there a woodcutter's shack and doesn't she remember a woodpile one could crouch behind to get out of the wind? There is no woodpile, no woodcutter's shack, but around the turn there are a carriage and a horse without a driver. The partly unharnessed horse hangs its head gloomily and dozes. The child doesn't hesitate for long; she sees that the leather top has been pulled back and climbs into the carriage, scoots all the way down and pulls the shiny black cover over her head. From this moment on everything is all right, the rushing of the wind through the pine tops a lullaby, the blood-red streak between the trees a friendly light. The child falls asleep as soon as she settles into the wagon, and her dreams are pleasant. Dreams of swinging: on a swing whose ropes are fastened God knows where, she soars above May-green birch groves. Suddenly, the swing stops; someone pulls on the ropes, it is dark again and a muzzle is pushed into the child's face. Her eyes snap open, but it doesn't help; the muzzle is a horse's mouth, but not a soft, round mouth like the mouth of the innkeeper's piebald; it's a mouth with long, yellow teeth, and wild, gleaming eyes extrude from the horse's head. Since the child does not remember how she got underneath the black oilcloth cover, it does not occur to her that the half-harnessed horse might have turned around to seek shelter and warmth where she is.

Because she is alone with the horse among the still black trees, the horse becomes the horror of horrors among all living creatures. Seeing it is worse than seeing her dead foster parents, a more ancient knowledge and therefore terrifying in a different way. The child slides past the horse's head and jumps out of the wagon; barefoot, she runs down cold, wet field lanes. The tambourine has been left behind and the horse's mouth must be thumping against the little calfskin, or how else could there be such strange, thudding sounds coming from the woods, but perhaps it is the heartbeat of the child who is running and running and whose every breath hurts her throat. At last she falls down and screams, hearing the horse's hoofbeats and the rolling of wheels behind her. But nothing happens, no carriage, no horse, and the sun has risen, and after a while someone calls out to the child, a woman from the neighborhood. The woman is out gathering kindling; she knows what has happened and takes the child home with her; eventually she is taken to an orphanage. Since that night she has never asked about her foster parents, though they were good to her and she was close to them. She has never gone near the house in which she lived. The more time passed the surer she became that she did not put the key into the tambourine but lost it somehow, and that she is therefore responsible for the deaths of her foster parents. But this has not weighed on her conscience. Other things happened to her before the good days finally began. She went through everything with a sort of cold courage, like someone who has been among the dead and returned to earth by some miracle. She is married now and has children of her own and lives an ordinary life with ordinary joys and sorrows. However, horses cause uncontrollable fear in the young woman, and I would not wish to see the panic in her eyes if she should ever hear the bells of a tambourine, which is unlikely.

Long Distance

◆

"Paul, it's me, Angeli," young Angelika Baumann told her
boyfriend Paul (on the phone). "I hope I'm not interrupting
you? Maybe you were working—good, I'm glad. I just wanted
to ask you if you had heard anything, I mean from your father . . . Sure. I'm impatient, I can't think of anything else. I
fantasize about it, our trip to see him—well, I'm a little scared,
too. You really think it will be all right with him? Oh, I hope
and pray. I want to like him so much, I want to like all your
relatives, especially your sister. I always wanted a sister of my
own . . . This weekend? Of course I'm free, it's what I've
been waiting for, this visit, and when it's all over we'll be engaged really and truly . . . No, don't laugh, Paul. You
shouldn't laugh, you don't understand . . . I took a walk in
the English Garden today and—what? Yes, it was a lovely day
for a walk, but I didn't see anything, I paid no attention to the
lilacs and the tulips . . . I kept sitting down on the benches,
and every time someone in the distance came towards me, it
was you. . . . And I thought about my life before I knew you
and how it wasn't really a life at all, and if you'd leave and I
never saw you again, I'd—O.K., I'm stupid, I admit it and I
won't say anything else. I really just called to find out if you
had heard from your father. So now I'll wait for the weekend.
It's my name day and maybe they'll give you to me as a present. 'Angeli, we give you our Paul. Make him happy' . . .
You're happy now? Oh Paul, don't say another word, you
couldn't say anything more beautiful. . . . On that I'm going
to hang up . . . ."

"Listen," the old man told his daughter Elly (on the phone), "you've got to talk turkey to your brother. It's not a matter of class prejudice. If she were someone special, with a reputation, say a movie actress or dancer, she could have grown up in the slums for all I'd care. But this one is nothing, working class, pure and simple, a pretty face as long as she's young, and later on, a butterball. No, I haven't met her, just looked at a snapshot—cute, and something soulful about the eyes. But those things don't last. Then comes the padding around the hips, and her hands are short and squat anyway. Paul simply can't go through with this, it's going to end badly, it'll be bad for everyone concerned. In a few years he's going to find her a social embarrassment. He is a pretty good businessman, and he has his Ph.D. Given a few years, he'll be a laughingstock with a wife who can't speak a single foreign language and thinks Picasso is a casserole from Provence. Invitations will be awkward, people won't want her, and he'll have to think up excuse after excuse: 'my wife is ill, my wife can't leave the children.' And one day a woman will sit next to him at dinner, a beautiful, well-dressed, quick-witted woman who lets him know that she is not indifferent to him, and he thinks, my God, if only I were free . . . So, do me a favor and tell Paul I don't want to get involved, but marriage is out of the question. You might call your Aunt Julia too. I think she's back from Gastein. We have to stick together, what's a family for . . . A family is powerful, even if we don't all live in the same town . . . that's what telephones were invented for. Quick, before I hang up, how are the kids? Don't let them up too soon; there can be complications after measles. Call me back, but not tomorrow night, I've got a business dinner, and the next night . . . Well, just keep trying, I'll be home some time or other."

"No doubt you can guess why I'm calling, Aunt Ju," Elly told her aunt Julia (on the phone). "Daddy wants you to get into this—you know, the older generation and all that. And of course it really is a stupid move, what Paul is planning . . . I always predicted that if he ever got married, it would be because someone got her hooks into him. Do I know her? Sure, I met her once. If you ask me, the iron fist in the velvet glove type, out to get what she wants, and I don't mean only our handsome boy. What you need to do is phone him, keep phoning him, or introduce him to another girl, you know so many people . . . Introduce him to someone and ask him to show her around Munich and take her to the theater at night, as a favor to you . . . That way he'll see there are other women in the world. What do you mean 'what if he loves her?' Come on, Aunt Ju, act your age. Who says he can't go on seeing her, sleep with her, if that's what he wants . . . Really, sometimes you sound positively medieval, if you'll forgive me for saying so. If you don't know what to say, tell him Daddy would be upset. His blood pressure is 200 as it is, and children are supposed to honor their parents. Coming from you, that wouldn't sound half-bad. Actually, Daddy is upset, he has certain expectations, and business may not be doing too well right now . . . Maybe he would like a wedding, but a posh one—engraved invitations and dinner at the Brenner Kurhof. It would cost him big bucks, but it might be worth it. Worries? Well, I don't know about that, maybe yes, maybe no, but I'm inclined to think he doesn't have any. Anyway, Aunt Ju, try not to be sentimental. The family has to stick together. My husband said he'd speak to Paul, too, man to man, when he has time, but of course he never does . . . ''

"No, nothing formal," Aunt Julia told her nephew Paul (on the phone), "just a few people for dinner. Lobster bisque, lamb chops with green beans, and dessert. You can go back the same night. Do your old aunt the favor. I need a table partner for a beautiful girl, reddish-blond hair, just your type. From South America, I mean she was born and raised there, but her parents are German and she is coming here to get acquainted with her old homeland. I thought you might help her out, you're such an expert when it comes to museums and galleries and theater and so on . . . Well, I know you said you were busy this weekend, but I won't accept that, you'll simply have to cancel your plans. You'll do this for me, won't you, dear? With your fiancée—that's the first I've heard of a fiancée! Well, no, to be truthful, I've heard something like that, but I didn't take it seriously. You are much too young to get married, and your father would not be pleased. I hope you aren't actually committed—I mean with an engagement ring or something like that. Not that that would be so important in our circles, but . . . Listen, Pauli, don't yell at me. Your nerves must be shot, of course I can understand that completely. This is tough for you. You are not a fighter, and there are bound to be obstacles. You really need to think the whole thing through again. Get to know the parents, I mean really well, especially the mother because the daughter will be like the mother twenty-five years from now. I know, I've observed that, I'm a person who thinks about things. No offense, I have nothing against the working class, and you are right, women are adaptable, but only up to a point. Well, I'll stop talking, and you be a good boy and come to my little dinner. Come a little early so we can talk some more. Incidentally, I hear your dad isn't feeling too well. Oh, and you can bring your fiancée, of course, but you'll have to let me know so I can invite an extra man. Cocktail dress, and I assume her French is good? The Belgian consul is coming, a lovely man, quite a collector, framed pictures of saints, just your cup of tea . . . ''

"Listen, Pauli," Elly told her brother (on the phone), "this business about your girl . . . Of course, everybody knows about it, and that you want to take her to see Daddy on Sunday . . . But I think you might want to postpone your visit a bit. Daddy has plans for you, he wants to give you a trip. He has already talked to your boss. You can take care of some business at the same time, so it won't be taken off your vacation. You really can't spoil Daddy's treat; there'll be plenty of time when you get back . . . Where to? I'm not quite sure—Canada, I think. No distance to speak of by plane. You could stop here on the way. The kids aren't contagious anymore and we'd love to see you. You could relax a bit and I could drive you out to the Elbe in my new red car, to Blankensee maybe. We can take a walk along the beach. Aunt Ju said you looked bad when you were at her place the other night, as if you

CIRCE'S MOUNTAIN

were under a lot of stress. Maybe it's all the business with the girl—is her name Angelika? Pretty name, and her last name? Baumann . . . and where in Munich does she live? No, no, I have no intention of visiting her; anyway, I couldn't leave here. I just want to give you some advice about—what? 'Leave her in the lurch,' don't be so melodramatic. Just remember how you talked me out of the singer I had such a crush on. By the way, I ran into him recently, and you have no idea how awful he looks now . . . I had to laugh and I'll be eternally grateful to you. Well O.K., maybe it isn't the same thing, but it's enough for me just to hear your voice, so tormented, not a trace of the old I-don't-give-a-damn-what-all-of-you-think spirit. That's the spirit you had at fourteen, when you wanted to run away from home to become a sailor or a dockworker, remember? Sure, it was awful at home, but kind of nice, too, and you've never been the type to rough it, then or now. At the time you didn't realize that, and I had to hide your shoes, but I bet you realize it now . . . Oh, I think you can imagine what I mean by roughing it: no more allowance, possibly no inheritance, depending on how pissed-off Daddy gets. Nobody said you picked her up off the street, of course not . . . What—a small notions and sundries store? Well, there you are—you'll have to go there for Sunday dinners, pork roast, red cabbage and apple pie in a rich crust . . . And at the wedding Daddy has to sit next to the notions and sundries mom and discuss the mark-up on rubber bands. Can you picture that scenario—frankly, I can't.''

"No, really, Angeli,'' Paul told his girlfriend (on the phone), "nothing is wrong, it's just that I'm sorry we can't go to Düsseldorf this weekend . . . things have come up . . . No, not as far as I'm concerned, but it doesn't work out for my dad, the two of us coming, I mean. I do have to go, he's got something to discuss with me. I'm supposed to take a business trip . . . No, just for a short time, for God's sake, it's nothing to cry about, and anyway, that's the way it's going to be, you might as well get used to it. I can't sit around home all the time! What do you mean 'in the beginning'?

When it was our secret . . . well, now they know and they'll just have to get used to it. Families always have other plans, and my family is no exception. Yes I *know* we used to go for a walk every night. Get off my back! Pretty soon you'll start asking me if I still love you . . . Of course I love you, the only time I'm happy is when we're together. That became clear to me when I went to Aunt Ju's for dinner, all I did was stare holes in the ceiling. I didn't say a word and Aunt Ju, who did her best to fix me up with another girl, finally raised her glass to me, which meant, 'I concede.' I'm telling you I have no commitment towards that girl, can't you believe me for God's sake and stop talking about 'my world'? I have a background like everybody else, but a world—that's what I want to find with you, maybe here, maybe somewhere else. No, no, I don't know where, not at this point . . . Listen, I've got to go. Say something nice before I hang up. That's not what I wanted to hear—what could you possibly be afraid of? Put on a record, our song, 'It Ain't Necessarily So' . . . I can't come by tonight, I'm leaving for Düsseldorf right after work, there's less traffic than tomorrow morning. My voice does *not* sound any different. You're imagining things. Sure there are difficulties, but that's no reason—yes, you are, you don't trust me, maybe you are too influenced by your parents. Why should I be in contact with your parents? I care about you, not your parents. If you keep this up—what did you say, Angeli? Say something, sweetheart, don't be mad, everything will work out . . . "

"Miss Baumann," Paul's sister Elly told Paul's girlfriend Angelika (on the phone), "you'll be surprised that I'm calling you, since I hardly know you . . . I'm not in Munich, I'm at home in Hamburg. No, there's nothing wrong, Paul is fine . . . Please calm down for a minute and listen to me, Miss Baumann. I don't know what Paul has told you about his family, assuming he has told you anything. Right now he may think he can get along without a family. But I think you might be interested in another opinion on that, namely that he needs his family and he can't get along without them. He shouldn't have to, you say, and you are right—I don't picture you as the kind of girl who sets her cap for a man, no matter what—see, that's what I thought. If I'd start raving about undying love to you, you'd laugh at me, right? I know young people aren't as romantic these days; they share a stretch of their lives and then they separate. I think that's wonderful—no sentimentality, each has his and her own life. What? It isn't true in your case? Well, maybe not in your case, Miss Baumann, but you must be aware of the fact that it's true for my brother . . . You're wrong, it's not our fault, it's not my father's doing. Actually, my father would very much like to speak to you. Perhaps you might wish to make a change, possibly move to another town, get away from home for a change . . . if so, you'll have expenses, which my father— there's no need to shout. I don't know what you're so excited about. Just in case, let me give you my father's address. Do you have a pencil . . . I'll wait. Hello? Düsseldorf-Büderich, Kastanienallee 42. He would be perfectly willing to visit you, but it might be best if you went to see him. I imagine you would like to see where Paul grew up . . . and of course you'll be reimbursed for your first-class train ticket . . . You want to go? Good, I'm delighted. But you sound so hostile. I don't think we should part like that, please Miss Baumann, don't hang up yet . . . ''

"That's very kind of you," Paul's father told his attorney, Dr. Kaminsky (on the phone), "a lot of work went into checking all that out, the compensation in case of a breach of promise suit, etcetera. Well, yes, that is what I asked for, but I think we may be able to postpone the whole matter for a while—in fact, it might not come to anything. Congratulations? What do you mean, aren't congratulations a bit premature? Oh, you mean for Paul—no, not a chance, Paul is not going to marry the girl. It wasn't hard to dissuade him, by the way, so it can't have been such a grand passion. You know, Kaminsky, he's too young; he doesn't really know what he wants yet. And no girl wants a weak, indecisive man. Deep down, what women really want isn't romance, but protection, I can vouch for that . . . Did you ask me if I know her? Of course I know her. After all, she came to see me. A pretty little thing, a bit prickly at first, a bit rebellious. But people like you and me, Kaminsky, we know how to handle women. She stayed all day Sunday and we drove to the Rhine and I showed her my collections . . . No, she's not stupid, not at all, very eager to learn, and there's something sweet about her, at least there was by the end of the visit. Badly dressed, of course. If it hadn't been Sunday, I would have liked to buy her something pretty. Well no, she probably wouldn't have let me . . . she didn't even accept reimbursement for her train fare.—So. I'll get back to you later. Right now things are still up in the air and I'd like to wait until Paul is back from Canada. I may drive down to Munich in the meantime; I have some other business there. Am I what? Come on, don't make me laugh. But she did like me, I could tell that much. And now you must excuse me—I've asked my coach to come during the lunch hour . . . of course, tennis, that'll keep me limbered up. Got to stay in shape, you know, and—here he is. Goodbye, Kaminsky, goodbye!"

"Aunt Ju," Paul's sister Elly told her Aunt Julia (on the phone), "I hope you weren't asleep yet . . . you were? Oh well, the phone is right next to your bed . . . I'm really sorry to be calling so late, but I had to ask you how you feel about Daddy going to Munich twice in the last ten days . . . Oh sure, to see the girl. Boy oh boy, what a schemer, and I'm the one who sent her to Düsseldorf in the first place! I could kick myself. But how was I to know anything like this would happen? Daddy is sixty-one, has had a heart attack, and he always said he wouldn't get over Mom. Yes, I think he intends to marry her. I can't be positive, of course, but I have that feeling. He takes no interest in us any more. You remember that matter concerning Erwin—Daddy had offered to speak to the Secretary of Commerce about it. It would be so helpful for us. Well, Erwin called to remind him and he just said, 'Yes, I know, but I'm too busy at the moment.' And Sibyl's birthday was this week—of course she got your package, thanks a million . . . You thought of her birthday, but Daddy forgot completely. He has always sent her a silver table setting for her birthday, she almost has a dozen now that she's turned ten. Well, of course I can remind him, but that's embarrassing, and anyway, this shows what we can expect if he marries again— and a twenty-two-year-old, who may want to have children of her own! No, I can't drive down there; the kids aren't back in school yet and besides, when I talked to her quite nicely on the phone the other day, she got nasty. As if it's our fault that Paul has pulled back. And she wouldn't admit that the young girls aren't as romantic these days either. Now we see how much there was to this grand passion and that all she wanted was to get into our family, and if she can't get the young man, the old one will do. Paul, yes, he has written, seems to be in good spirits, probably glad to be away, but of course he has no idea what's been going on here . . . A telegram? I wouldn't think of it. We'd make ourselves ridiculous, and anyway, once Daddy has decided to do something, there's no one can stop him, least of all his children—though you might be able to, Aunt Julia. Promise me you'll call him. Right away. Sure. Tell him that, tell him he's an old fool. That's the right approach."

"Let me see," Angelika Baumann told her friend Renate (on the phone), "it will be three months tomorrow. Why Düsseldorf? Because this is where my husband lives. You heard right, I married an old man with lots of money, just like we used to say we were going to, and then we laughed and said we'd never make it. Well—it turns out I did make it. Yes, a widower. Two children. A grown daughter . . . and a son, also grown, a businessman like his dad. Me, fall for the son? Not a chance. What do you care what the son looks like? He doesn't live in town and doesn't intend to move here either . . . And my husband's daughter doesn't come to see us. There's also an aunt, but my husband wants nothing to do with any of his family. He even stopped their allowances. Me? No, he doesn't treat me like that; in fact, he spoils me. Lovely house, brand-new swimming pool in the backyard. And he

talks about buying me a house in Tessin and a sports car, just
for my use . . . Oh sure, I'm enjoying life, especially because
the family resents the fact that I'm pregnant and my baby will
inherit everything . . . Well, maybe that doesn't sound like
the me you remember, but circumstances alter cases, certain
circumstances . . . I can't expect you to understand. I have
to stop talking now and change clothes. Some people are coming to dinner, including a senator. Let me know if you need
anything. Getting together—I'm not sure that's such a good
idea. You have a good memory . . . yes I did have a
boyfriend I couldn't marry because his family was against it
and he wouldn't stand up to them. No . . . I haven't forgotten him, but that's no reason—I mean that's exactly the
reason—what do you mean, my voice? You're always imagining things. As if I had any reason to cry . . . ''

Thaw

The apartment was on the second floor of a large, bright building. The rooms, too, were bright and friendly: blue linoleum with white speckles, a glass-fronted walnut cabinet, a foam rubber armchair upholstered in brilliant red. The kitchen was old-fashioned but freshly painted, snowy white and cozy, with a banquette and a large table. Outside, it was thawing; the snow was melting; it dripped from the gutter and slid down the gable roof in large chunks, whirling past the window. The woman was in the kitchen when the man came home from work. It was beginning to get dark; it was almost 6 o'clock. She heard him unlock the apartment door from the outside, lock it again from the inside, walk into the bathroom, open the door behind her and say hello. Then she finally lifted her hands out of the soapy broth in which two long stockings were winding like eels, shook the drops from her fingers, turned around and nodded at him.

"Did you lock the door?" she asked.

"Yes," the man answered.

The woman went to the window and let down the shutter. "Don't turn the light on yet," she said. "There's a crack in the shutter. It would be best if you could nail a piece of cardboard against it."

"You are too fearful," the man said.

He went out and came back with some tools and a piece of heavy cardboard. Someone had glued a picture to one side of the cardboard, a black man with a red bandanna and gleaming teeth, and the man nailed the cardboard so that the black man faced into the kitchen. He worked by the scanty light that fell into the kitchen from the hall, and as soon as he was finished the woman went and turned out the hall light and closed the door. The neon tube above the stove flickered and jerked; suddenly the room was brilliantly lit, and the man walked over to the sink to wash his hands and sat down at the table.

"I'd like to eat now," he said.

"Yes," the woman said.

She took a platter of sliced ham, sausage and dill pickles out of the refrigerator and added a bowl of potato salad. Bread was already on the table, in an attractive woven basket sitting on a linen-look oilcloth that was patterned with cheerful little boats.

"Did you bring the paper?" the woman asked.

"Yes," the man said. He went back out to the hall, returned and placed the newspaper on the table.

"You have to close the door," the woman said. "The light shines right through the glass door; anyone on the stairs can see that we're at home. What does the paper say?" she asked.

"Something about the dark side of the moon," the man said. He had closed the door and sat down again and was now starting in on the potato salad and sausage. "And something about China and Algiers."

"I didn't mean that," the woman said. "I want to know if the police are going to do anything."

"Yes," the man said. "They've drawn up a list."

"A list," the woman said sarcastically. "Did you see any police on the street?"

"No," the man said.

"Not even in front of the Red Stag at the corner?"

"No," the man said.

The woman had seated herself at the table and was eating a little of the food, all the time listening anxiously for any sound that came from the street outside.

"I don't understand you," the man said. "I can't imagine who would want to harm us, and why."

"I know who," the woman said.

"Besides *him*, I mean," the man said, "and he is dead."

"I'm quite sure," the woman said.

She got up, cleared away the dishes, and immediately

started washing them, trying to make as little noise as possible. The man lit a cigarette and stared at the front page of the paper, but it was obvious that he wasn't reading.

"We were always good to him," he said.

"That doesn't make any difference," the woman said.

She took the stockings from the washbowl, rinsed them and hung them up above the radiator with blue plastic clothespins.

"Do you know how they do it?" she asked.

The man said, "No, and I don't want to know either. I'm not afraid of those bastards. I want to listen to the news."

"They ring the bell," the woman said, "but only if they know there's someone at home. If no one answers they smash the glass and come in with their guns drawn."

"Lay off," the man said. "Hellmuth is dead."

The woman removed the towel that hung on a plastic hook on the wall and dried her hands.

"I have to tell you something," she said. "I didn't want to tell you before, but now I've got to. When I was picked up by the police . . . "

Startled, the man put down the paper and looked at his wife. "Yes?" he asked.

"They took me to the morgue," the woman said, "and a policeman started to uncover one of the bodies, but slowly, starting at the feet.

'Are those your son's shoes?' he asked me, and I answered, "Yes, those are his shoes."

'And are these his clothes?' the policeman asked next, and I said, 'Yes, these are his clothes.' "

"I know," the man said.

" 'And is that his face?' he finally asked me and pulled back the sheet, but just for a moment because the face was so devastated and he was afraid I would faint.

'Yes,' I said, "that's his face.' "

"I know," the man said.

The woman walked to the table, sat down opposite her husband and rested her head on her hands.

"I did not recognize him," she said.

Thaw

"Nevertheless, it could have been him," the man said.

"But not necessarily," the woman said. "I came home and told you it was him and you were glad."

"Both of us were glad," the man said.

"Because he was not our son," the woman said.

"Because he was like he was," the man said.

He stared at his wife's face, an eternally young, round face, ringed by curls, which was capable of changing without warning into the face of a very old woman.

"You look tired," he said. "You are nervous; we should go to sleep."

"It's no use," the woman said. "We haven't been able to sleep for ages. We just pretend and silently open our eyes, and when morning comes, our silent eyes look at each other."

"Adopting a child is probably always a bad idea," the man said. "We made a mistake, but it's all right now."

"I did not recognize the dead man," the woman said.

"He may be dead anyway," the man said, "or out of the country, in America or Australia, far away."

At that moment another large chunk of snow slid off the roof and hit the pavement with a soft, dull thud.

"Do you remember that Christmas with all the snow," the woman said.

"Yes," the man said. "Hellmuth was seven. We bought him a toboggan, and he got a lot of other presents, too."

"But not what he wanted," the woman said. "He rummaged through all the presents and searched and searched for something."

"Eventually he calmed down and played with the blocks. He built a house without windows and doors and put a high wall around it."

"And that spring he choked the rabbit to death," the woman said.

"Let's talk about something else," the man said. "Hand me the broom so I can fix the handle."

"That makes too much noise," the woman said. "Do you know what they call themselves?"

"No," the man said, "and I don't care to know. I want to go to bed or do something."

"They call themselves The Judges," the woman said.

She froze and listened; someone was coming up the stairs. The someone stopped for a moment, and then walked on, all the way to the top floor.

"You are driving me crazy," the man said.

"When he was nine he hit me for the first time," the woman said, "remember?"

"I remember," the man said. "He had been kicked out of school and you were reproaching him. That's when he was sent to reform school."

"He came home for summer vacation," the woman said.

"He came home for summer vacation," the man repeated. "One Sunday I took him to the lakes in the woods. We saw a spotted salamander. On the way home he held my hand."

"Next day he beat up the mayor's son and made him lose an eye," the woman said.

"He didn't know it was the mayor's son," the man said.

"It was awfully embarrassing," the woman said. "You came this close to losing your job."

"We were glad when that vacation ended," the man said. He got up, took a bottle of beer from the refrigerator and put a glass on the table. "How about you?" he asked.

"No thanks," the woman said. "He didn't love us."

"He didn't love anybody," the man said, "but he did come to us for protection once."

"He had run away from the institution," the woman said. "He didn't know where else to go."

"The director called us," the man said. "He was a cheerful, friendly gentleman. He told us not to open the door if Hellmuth showed up. He pointed out that he had no money and wouldn't be able to buy any food. When a bird is hungry it returns to its cage."

"Is that what he said?" the woman asked.

"Yes," the man said. "And he wanted to know if Hellmuth had friends in the area."

"But he didn't," said the woman.

"The snow was melting at the time," the man said. "It was sliding down the roof and onto the balcony in big clumps."

"Like tonight," the woman said.

"Exactly like tonight," the man said.

"Exactly like tonight," the woman repeated. "We darkened the window and whispered and pretended we were not at home. The child climbed up the stairs and rang the bell and knocked."

"Hellmuth wasn't a child anymore," the man said. "He was fifteen and we had to do what the director told us to."

"We were afraid," the woman said.

The man poured himself another glass of beer. The street noises were almost inaudible now, but they could hear strong gusts of wind, a south wind blowing up from the mountains.

"He knew," the woman said. "He was fifteen, but he stood on the stairs and cried."

"That's all in the past," the man said and began running his middle finger between the boats on the oilcloth, back and forth, without touching any of them.

"There was a gypsy woman in the police station," the woman said. "Her child was dead, run over. She screamed like an animal."

"The blood speaking," her husband said derisively. He looked distressed.

"He did have a friend once," the woman said. "A small, weak boy. They tied him to a post in the schoolyard and set the grass around his feet on fire. Since it was a hot day, the grass burned."

"There you have it again," the man said.

"No," the woman said, "Hellmuth wasn't involved, he wasn't even there. The boy was able to break loose, but in the end he died. All the boys went to his funeral and scattered flowers on the grave."

"Hellmuth too?" the man asked.

"No, not Hellmuth," the woman answered.

"He had no heart," the man said, rolling the empty glass between his hands.

"I'm not so sure about that," the woman said.

"It's so bright in here," the man said suddenly. He stared at the neon tube above the stove and then he placed one hand over his eyes and rubbed his closed lids.

"Where's the picture?" he asked.

"I put it in the cabinet," the woman said.

"When?" the man asked.

"A long time ago," the woman answered.

"When exactly?" the man asked again.

"Yesterday," the woman answered.

"Does that mean you saw him yesterday?" the man asked.

"Yes," the woman said quickly, as if it were a relief. "He was at the corner, in front of the Red Stag."

"Alone?" the man asked.

"No," the woman said. "With a bunch of guys I didn't know. They were hanging out with their hands in their pockets, not talking. Then they heard something that I heard, too, a long, shrill whistle, and they vanished as if the earth had swallowed them."

"Did he see you?" asked the man.

"No," the woman said. "I got off the streetcar and he had his back to me."

"Maybe it wasn't him," the man said.

"I can't be absolutely sure," the woman said.

The man got up, stretched, yawned and tapped against the chair leg with his foot several times.

"That's why people shouldn't adopt kids. You can't predict how they'll turn out."

"You can't predict how anybody will turn out," the woman answered.

She opened a drawer, reached inside and took out a spool of black thread and a sewing needle.

"Take off your jacket," she said. "The top button is loose."

While the man took off his jacket he watched her trying to thread the needle. The kitchen was bright and the eye of the needle large, but her hands trembled, and she could not do it. He put the jacket on the table, and his wife tried to thread the needle again and again, without success. "Read me something," she begged when she noticed that he kept watching her.

"From the paper?" the man asked.

"No," the woman said, "from a book."

The man went to the living room and immediately returned with a book. As he put it on the table he searched his pockets for his glasses; then both of them heard the cat crying outside the window.

"There she is, home at last, the little run-around," the man said, getting up and trying to lift the shutter a little, but it wouldn't budge because of the cardboard.

"You'll have to take down the cardboard," the woman said.

The man took a pair of pliers and pulled the nail out of the cardboard. He raised the shutter and the cat jumped down from the windowsill and streaked across the kitchen like a pitch-black shadow.

"Should I nail the cardboard back?" the man asked, and the woman shook her head. "I wish you'd read now," she said. The man leaned the cardboard with the black man against the refrigerator, and the black man beamed at him from below. Then he sat down and pulled his glasses from their case.

"Kitty," he said, and the cat jumped on his lap and purred, and he ran his hand across its back and suddenly looked quite relaxed.

"Please read," his wife said.

"From the beginning?" the man asked.

"No," the woman said. "Start anywhere. Open the book anywhere and read."

"That doesn't make sense," the man said.

"Yes it does," the woman said. "I want to find out if we are guilty."

The man put on his glasses and leafed through a bunch of pages. The book was a random choice; he had grabbed it in the dark; they didn't have many books. "But now I was a ghost when I saw him," he read slowly and clumsily, "for his regular but strong features, the black curls that fell on his brow, the large eyes lit by cold fires—all this I continued to see before me as if it had been a painted portrait." He read a few more words and dropped the book on the table and said, "This tells us nothing."

"No," the woman said, and again she held the needle against the light with her left hand and guided the black thread past the eye with her right.

"Why do you have to know?" the man asked. "Every human being is guilty and not guilty; there's no point in thinking about it."

"If we are guilty," the woman said, "we have to open the shutter so everyone can see that we are home. And we have to turn on the light in the hall and unlock the apartment door so that whoever wants to come in, can."

The man made a gesture of impatience, and the cat jumped down from his lap and slinked towards the corner with the garbage can, where a bowl of milk stood waiting. The woman had stopped trying to thread the needle; she had put her head on the table, on top of her husband's jacket, and it was so quiet that all they heard was the sound of the cat drinking and licking its bowl in the corner.

"Is that what you want?" the man asked.

"Yes," the woman said.

"Even the apartment door?" the man asked.

"Yes," the woman said.

"But you aren't sure it was him at the corner by the Red Stag," the man objected. But he was already getting up and raising the shutter all the way, and he noticed all the others were down and the glow of the neon light beamed out into the night like the white fire of a lighthouse.

"It's certainly possible," he said, "that it was Hellmuth who got killed in that knife fight and that his face got smashed."

"Yes, it's possible," the woman said.

"And?" the man asked.

"It's beside the point," the woman said.

The man went into the hall and turned on the light, and

then he unlocked the door to the apartment. When he returned, the woman lifted her face from the scratchy jacket; the herringbone pattern was on her cheek and she was smiling at him.

"Anybody could walk in," he said disapprovingly.

"Yes," the woman said, and her smile became even more tender.

"Now they don't have to go to the trouble of smashing the glass," the man said. "They can simply walk in and suddenly appear in the kitchen with their guns."

"Yes," the woman said.

"And what are we going to do now?" the man asked.

"We wait," the woman said.

She reached out and pulled her husband down beside her on the banquette. The man sat down and put on his jacket, and the cat jumped on his lap.

"You can turn the radio on now," the woman said. The man reached over towards the buffet and pushed a button; the radio's green eye came on and the call letters lit up. There was music that was strange and didn't really sound much like music, and any other evening the man would have turned the dial to the right or the left, but tonight he didn't care and didn't move. Nor did the woman move; she had put her head on the man's shoulder and closed her eyes. He, too, closed his eyes, because the light blinded him and because he was very tired. Crazy, he thought, we sit in the lighthouse and wait for the killer, even though it may not have been our boy at all; our boy may be dead. He noticed that his wife was dropping off and decided that as soon as she was sound asleep he would get up, lower the shutter and lock the door. But she had not slept on his shoulder for a long time, not for years, and now she was doing it just the way she used to and acting as she used to, except that her face had some wrinkles, but he didn't notice her face and white hair. And since everything was as it used to be, he was reluctant to withdraw his shoulder; besides, she might wake up and the whole thing would start all over again. All over again, he thought, from the beginning; we wanted a child. I always wanted a child and nothing hap-

CIRCE'S MOUNTAIN

pened; that one, Sister, the curlyhead in the third row, and don't I hear someone on the stairs, a boy? Don't open, the director said, shhh, still as mice. Still as mice. We did not love him; the curlyhead has turned into a wild animal; come on in, gentlemen, all the doors are open, go ahead and shoot, it's what my wife wants, and it doesn't hurt. "It doesn't hurt," he said out loud, half asleep, and the woman opened her eyes and smiled, and then both of them slept and did not notice later, that the cat jumped down and disappeared through the slightly open window, that the snow slid from the roof and the window stirred in the warm breeze and that finally it was dawn. They slept, leaning against each other, deeply and calmly, and no one came to kill them; in fact no one came at all the whole night long.

Christine

◆

The way my husband has been acting lately, it's hard for me
to describe. The way he sits there absolutely motionless in the
middle of the room and looks through you as if there was
nothing there, not even a body with arms and legs and a dress
and an apron, not to mention his own wife. "George," I say,
trying to make my voice sound humorous, "don't stare holes
in the air, why not go out in the garden, the roses need to be
covered, there's supposed to be frost tonight." Of course I
could do that myself, or send one of the children outside, but
I'm not one of these wives who assign their husbands all sorts
of chores. He has never washed a dish in his life. But I don't
like the fact that he calls in sick when he isn't sick at all and is
sitting around the house getting silly ideas, because I know
what those ideas are. Not what you think, although, yes, in a
way what you think, but it's not that simple, not that
commonplace—

The simple, the commonplace, is a man of about fifty, a
father of four children, the wife a little bulky around the hips,
and he can't imagine ever having been crazy with love, and if
he remembers, he's embarrassed. But to be crazy with love
again, that's what he wants, once more in his life, if only in his
head—yes, better in his head, because it's all so complicated;
the wife watches, and the children watch; the children are
grown. Men get ideas like that on the beach, sitting there with
the whole family and the picnic basket, and they see the
young women on the diving board. Or else when it's evening
and the stores are closing, they look out the window and see
the young women walking arm in arm down the street. That's
how it is with a man of around fifty; it passes, you don't have

to get upset about it, and the best thing is to act as if you didn't notice anything. But I do get upset when my husband stands at the window, and even more when he sits in the middle of the room, without a newspaper, without anything. I get upset because I know what's behind it in his case, and that it isn't fear of getting old, but a certain specific recollection.

"Do what you can, Mrs. Bornemann, to make your husband forget the whole thing as quickly as possible," the doctor said at the time, our family doctor, whom we really had only for the children, since the two of us were never sick. After all we were still young, thirty-eight and thirty-two, and the kids were small. My husband was already working for Gütermann, and he's still there. But we didn't live here then, we lived in a sort of suburban slum, one of those developments of little row houses that fall apart before they are completed. Soon after what happened happened—I'll tell about it in a minute—soon afterwards we moved away, I insisted on it; it wasn't any good always looking out on the small front yard and the bed of asters and the fence posts the child had clung to, her hands blue from the cold, with a strand of her white-blond hair caught on the fence for a long time and no one having nerve enough to pull it out and throw it away.

Now you must be thinking it was one of our children whose hair was caught out there on the fence and whom my husband can't forget. But it was not one of our children. All our children have thrived; they've always been in fine physical shape and good in school and a source of pleasure for us. Yes, for my husband, too, and he never used to look at them the way he looks at them now sometimes, with such indifference and reluctance and sometimes even with an expression of revulsion, the way one looks at an animal, an unwanted, repellent animal—

That was about ten days ago, yes, exactly ten days ago. It was a Sunday, and since we have a car now we often drive somewhere for the whole day, even though we'd really rather stay home sometimes and the kids would prefer to sleep late and spend the afternoon with their friends. At breakfast we discuss where to go, and right away the arguments start. The boys are sleepy and in a bad mood, and the girls are covered with face cream because according to them their skin has to relax on Sundays. The kids are all sprawling and yawning, and my husband has the map in front of him and suggests this or that place, and someone always has an objection, one place has no water, another no woods, this one is too boring, that one too quiet. I try to make peace, and also I nag the kids about talking with their mouths full and throwing their wadded-up napkins on the table. But I don't take those things too seriously, and my husband never took them too seriously either, only on this particular day everything irritated and bothered him. He said something about dirty fingernails, and that Judith is too fat to wear slacks. Naturally, the kids talked back; Beppo explained that he couldn't be expected to have clean fingernails as long as he had to lug the coal upstairs, and Judith said, "Where do you think I get the upholstery, Mom is pretty well padded around the hips herself." That's true, and it's a fact that the kids are chubby and don't have good figures, and that they have plump hands and broad faces. But that's hardly their fault. It's not their fault, and it's no reason to do what my husband did that day. Which was to get up and throw down the map and yell, "For this, for this!" and to run out of the room as if he were crazy.

Of course by now I know exactly what those words, *for this, for this,* were all about. But at that time I didn't know. I remained at the table and calmed the children down, though I must say they weren't all that affected and Uwe, the youngest, even mumbled something like "not quite all there." That was insolent, and it hurt me all the more because I felt something really was out of kilter. Eventually we drove off by ourselves, without the children, that Sunday. We took a walk in the woods and stopped for coffee. My husband was silent and depressed the whole time. When we were sitting in the café in the woods, where a bunch of carefree young people had gathered for an afternoon of boating and dancing, he began observing the girls, not like someone looking for a fling, but soberly and with attention, as if he were looking for someone, some particular person. And then a young woman walked by our table, holding hands with a young man the way they do these days, a young woman with loose white-blond hair and a pale, almost translucent face. My husband raised his head and looked carefully at the girl, and then he dropped his face in his hands and said, "Exactly like her," in a voice that sounded broken and harsh and desperate. And all of a sudden I knew what he meant and why that morning he had said, *for this, for this,* and that all my efforts had been for nothing.

All my efforts, that sounds so solemn, like careful plans and intentions. But I never did have specific intentions and did not lay out any plan. "Out," I thought to myself, "out of this apartment, this neighborhood, away from the people we know, to the other side of town." That was a goal and something to do, and later I looked for other goals and other things to do. I wasn't interested in money, didn't mind the small, shabby apartment, and I wasn't ambitious for my husband, just so he earned enough to pay for the children's education. But at this point I started pushing, saying he should try to get ahead, move into a managerial position. So he spent his evenings studying, and he enjoyed that. When a few years later he actually did become a department head and we celebrated his promotion that evening with a glass of wine, even woke up the children and let them clink glasses and toast him, I thought again of our family doctor back in the old development days, and I looked at my husband and thought, he has forgotten about it, it's behind us. But now I know that we never put it behind us. Because the words, *for this, for this* meant: for these children, for this woman, for this family life I have taken upon myself a guilt no one can ever absolve me of. And when my husband said, *exactly like her,* apropos of the beautiful, delicate girl in the outdoor cafe, he was thinking of the child who was murdered in front of our garden gate and who had cried out for help so pitifully.

Of course it's not a question of my husband's guilt. If anyone is to blame, it's me. I told my husband this a hundred times when the police came and he had something like a breakdown, glazed eyes, trembling hands and froth coming from his mouth. I told the police the same thing, and they tried to calm my husband down and said we would probably be asked to appear as witnesses, nothing more, and of course we did appear as witnesses at the trial and no one blamed my husband in any way. All we had to do was tell how it was, such and such, my husband was home that day because he had been sick, not like now, but really sick. It's his first day out of bed and he's standing at the window and I'm clearing the table and glancing out the window too just then. The child comes running down the sidewalk, a thin child with white-blond hair, unknown to us, and a large, heavy man, also unknown to us, is right behind her. The child sees us, or at least my husband, and starts to scream and rattle our garden gate, which is locked, and the large, heavy man throws himself on the child, reaches under the white hair from behind and puts his hands around her throat. Between the child's first cry and her eventual silence there is an interval of a few minutes during which my husband turns around and starts to run out the door, which he can't because I cling to him and dig my fingers like claws into his sleeves and he cannot shake me off. "Don't go," I say, hoarse with fear and alarm, "think of the children, don't go." And because I say that, my husband, who might have got away, stops for a moment, just long enough for the stranger out there to squeeze the screaming little bird's throat shut. We recounted all this at the trial and learned a number of things, that the child's name was Christine and that she was seven and had only been living on our street for a few days. We also found out that the man, the murderer, was insane and imagined the whole world was persecuting him, and that he had been made fun of by an entirely different child a few minutes earlier and thought he had to revenge himself or protect himself against some unspecified threat. But I'm asking you—what business of ours was all this really?

"What business of yours is it," I said to my husband, and I also said that a lot of children die young, that they are run over or catch polio or t.b.; children die and adults die, there's no end to it; every second someone dies in this world. Every second someone takes his last breath, and if he doesn't cling to the posts of a garden fence, he clings to a sheet or the earth or the hand that tries to wipe away the perspiration. "She was fated to die young," I say, and who knows what might have happened to her, something much worse, and even though I myself carried the child into the house and held her panic-stricken, distorted little face against me, I'm still of the same opinion. I imagine there are people who blame me for that, but I can't help it if my husband is dearer to me than a strange little girl named Christine. I can't help it that throughout the trial I saw only his pale, helpless face and that I was full of anger and could think of nothing except, why did this have to happen to us? Why did the child have to walk on our side of the street when she lived on the other side, the side with the even numbers, and why did the madman have to catch up with her right in front of our garden gate? Why did it have to be a day on which my husband was at home, and why did we have to be in the living room even though we are usually in the kitchen at that hour? Why did everything have to happen in such a way that my husband can't get rid of the idea that he could have saved the child . . .

Because I know now that nothing, not his rise in the company, not homeownership and the good life, has been able to dispel this thought in him. I know that he hates me because I would not let him go that day, and that he hates the children because they are alive and healthy and strong. Since that Sunday drive to the woods I've been watching him constantly, and sometimes I'm so angry I want to shake him. Wake up! I want to shout, such dreams are sick: where would we be if we let everything touch us so deeply? I can see where: in a state of loneliness and depression, of not being quite 'all there,' because being 'all there' means taking everything as it comes and making the best of it, and not hanging on to a ghost, the ghost of someone you didn't even know and who has been dead for ten years now.

But there are times when I think it isn't really guilt that stalks and tortures my husband. I think that for him the dead child represents a pure state of grace and beauty, and because she died so young and had no real contact with the world she remained like that, so graceful and so innocent. And then I admit in private that for women everything must make sense and have a reason, but that men hold on to a dream and so have a right to be sad about the insanity and disorder of the world. I admit this, in private, now as I step into the garden, and there is my husband, and he actually has covered the roses with pine boughs and old gunny sacks, and now he is looking at the birch, which has been infested by some pest that causes the leaves to curl, and he has an unhappy expression on his face. I watch him and I love him more than ever in my life, even more than during the first years of our marriage. But I wouldn't dare tell him that. So I simply put my hand on his arm, very lightly, and say, "Thank you," and he turns around, surprised but not unfriendly.

X Day

I think you know what day I mean by that. X stands for A, as in annihilation, not of the whole world exactly, but something similar, our city gone, every house, school, library, every man, woman and child, everything we lived for, and while there may still be human beings crawling around somewhere, they won't for long, and anything born afterwards has been killed off prematurely.

X Day is on my mind, I keep thinking about it, but I'm the only one in my family and among my friends who does. Nor am I supposed to mention it—don't talk like that, they say right away, it's not going to happen, and if it does we'll find out soon enough. Because I can't talk about it I have to write it down, describe X Day, which like any other day has a beginning and like any other day goes on, as you'll see. Of course I have no idea what the weather will be like on this day, but let's assume fine weather, let's assume summer has turned and the sunflowers are blooming. We are not entirely unprepared, there is an atmosphere of crisis, political crisis, as we've known it before, in fact known it often at this time of year.

I wake up early on this day, peer at the clear September sky through the slit between the drapes and then look at the clock. It is seven, I could let my husband sleep for another half hour, but because of the premonition I have I don't do that. Instead I wake him up gingerly, saying, "It's still early for you, but it's a question of the children, I mean whether they should go to school or not." My husband sits up in bed and rubs his eyes. "Why," he asks, "why shouldn't they go to school, are they sick or is there an epidemic at their school, you could have mentioned that yesterday, but you didn't say anything." "Because," I reply, "there is no epidemic and the children aren't sick and because last night I didn't know what I know now, namely that this is our last day, and I think we should be together."

"Our last day," my husband repeats with surprise, "what do you mean," and then he starts laughing and says, "Don't let them drive you crazy, the situation will straighten out, after all everyone knows that it's a futile undertaking and there are no winners and losers in the end."

"You keep saying that," I say, sitting on the edge of the bed and pulling on my stockings, "and it may be true, but it isn't necessarily true—I mean that everyone knows that and acts accordingly, and today we've reached the end, this is our last day."

My husband looks at me sideways, a kind enough look, and suggests that we take the newspaper out of the mailbox, and I already know the paper will be no help because nothing has happened as long as "it" hasn't happened and because no newspaper in the world will tell you, you must die, be prepared.

"So you see," my husband says after getting the paper and reading excerpts to me, the text of cables and even telephone conversations between the superpowers, "they see a way out, they're going to find one, and by the way I woke up the children."

"But surely they're not going to school," I say, "and you, for my sake please don't go to the office." "Of course I'm going," my husband, who works for the national railroad, says, "and so are the kids, how are you going to explain to them why they shouldn't go," and he plugs in his electric razor, which has quite a loud hum, and I know he can't hear me anymore.

At this point I'm fully dressed, and I go into the children's room, which is usually gloomy at this hour; either the kids are still in bed and you have to pull off their covers, or they've skipped their baths and are already dressed and have their

CIRCE'S MOUNTAIN

math or language notebooks open, saying, "Leave us alone, we don't have time for breakfast this morning."

The kids, two boys of ten and twelve, act their age and are hardly demonstrative, I can't expect a good morning kiss anymore. That they should run up to me and hug me on this particular day, breaks my heart. "Why," I say breathlessly, "Why did you get up today when there's no school?" "No school," the oldest says, "you've got to be off your rocker," that's how he expresses himself, tapping his forehead with his finger. And then it turns out that his schedule today calls for two hours of films, while in the day of the younger one something is obviously afoot, a plan to sneak off for a smoke during break or God knows what—anyway, an interesting day, a day not to be missed.

"But there isn't any school today," I say bravely and start to make the beds in order to avoid the boys' eyes. "How do you know," says Arno, the older one, and I say, "That's what I heard," and immediately regret the whole thing, afraid the children might catch on. But Arno merely says, "I think I'd better phone," in a neutral voice, and he starts to walk through the door, so that I have a hard time keeping him back with a hasty, "No, never mind, you're probably right." Arno shakes his head and thinks something about women, and so does my husband, and after a stormy breakfast, when the children have left, he articulates it. "How strange you are today," he says, "I don't know you like this," because tears are running down on my toast with honey, and I've not yet fixed my hair.

"You're right," I say, "I don't know myself like this either, but that's precisely the reason why there must be something to it, and no one believed Cassandra either." And since I'm on the subject of antiquity, I tell my husband about the dead of Pompeii, recast according to the impressions they left in the lava, whom one can admire in the museum in their pitiful stances of flight, or else mourn as human beings surprised by death. And finally I say, "That's how it's going to be for us."

My husband is bothered by this story. He gives me a look

of annoyance and drinks his coffee very fast, and it's a good thing the telephone rings just then; normally I answer, but this time my husband picks up the receiver. "Yes, it's me," he says happily, "No, I'm still here, I can pick you up, I'll be glad to. You'll be waiting outside, but that's not necessary, we have plenty of time." I'm wondering who it might be, a colleague or a secretary; at any rate a voice from life, a voice that says we go on, everything goes on, today and tomorrow, there is no such thing as death.

"Well, you must excuse me," my husband says and gives me a kiss, "and don't think about such gruesome things, it only gets you down, you are pale enough already." He promises to call me as soon as he hears any news, and then he says goodbye and takes the car keys off the hook in the hall, and I hear the keys rattling softly as on any other morning, and his quick steps down the stairs as on any other morning, and for a moment I feel reassured, he is right, I drive myself crazy, I drive everybody crazy.

I spend the morning as I do every morning. We live comfortably, but we have no help. So I make the beds as usual and dust as usual, and then I go shopping, keeping my ears open for what people in the stores are saying. But they are saying the usual things, great fall weather we're having, how was your vacation, the apples are still sky-high, and when I try to change the subject to the political situation, they are suddenly in a big hurry, excuse me, I have to go to the fishmarket, I must go pick up my aunt at the train, I'm due at the beauty salon. Of course I barely know the people who say these things and rush off, but I do know the man at the streetcar stop, he is the minister from whom my kids take religious instruction. He doesn't like clerical garb, he is wearing a beret, but that doesn't keep me from asking him a spiritual question. "Good morning, Reverend," I say, and he says, "Hello, Mrs. Reiter. How are the boys, out on a field trip I hope, who knows how long this beautiful weather will hang on, this may be the last day." "Yes," I say, shaken, "the last day, you may be right, and what shall we do Reverend, I'm asking you what shall we do?"

The minister looks at me with surprise, but he isn't stupid, he senses something, so he says, "You mustn't worry, Mrs. Reiter, we are all in God's hands." "But worry is just what I need to do," I say. Except that by that time the streetcar comes charging up to the stop, a certain gentleman doffs his beret and jumps on the already crowded steps, a clergyman who is full of life, that's what he is, and he hurries from here to there, always on the go. Everyone is full of life, my family and the housewives and the minister, everyone except me, though I just bought a piece of veal shoulder and half a pound of mushrooms, you can guess what's on my mind, a kind of last supper, with a sweet dessert, but perhaps I simply want to distract myself and anyway it's getting late. I get home just before 12 o'clock, thinking that my husband might have tried to call me; at this moment he's in a meeting, but it might be best if I phoned him, although he doesn't like being called out of a meeting, hates it in fact.

"What's the problem," he says when I finally have him on the phone, sounding irritated, and I say, "Nothing. But I've been running late and I thought I might have missed your call." "My call," my husband says, surprised, "why should I call," and I ask the question which happens to come to my mind and seems extraordinarily important to me, "Are the trains running?" I ask in a trembling voice. "My dear child," my husband says, "how would I know, we aren't meeting in the train station, of course the trains are running, why do you ask, are you thinking of taking a trip or what."

"Just in general," I say and hang up. Half an hour passes, during which I'm busy in the kitchen, repeating my husband's words to myself, words that sound reassuring one minute and extremely disturbing the next. Finally I can stand it no longer and take off for school, Gutenberg School, which both children attend. It so happens that the principal is standing at the front entrance talking to the janitor; it seems the banister is loose and needs fixing: the principal rattles the iron posts and has a worried look on his face.

"Hello," I say, "evidently you didn't think it necessary to send the children home, you've probably received some encouraging news, that's good." "Why should I send the children home," the principal asks, surprised. He looks at me as if I'd lost my mind and I say quickly, "Why indeed, you're quite right." I walk past him and he stares after me suspiciously, as does the janitor, but they can't stop me from entering the building and picking up my two boys, it's almost time for the last bell. In fact a bunch of kids are coming out of the gym; I recognize my oldest boy and turn red with happiness—if it happens now, I think, at least we've seen each other once more.

My boy hurries past me with the others, but when they have turned the corner he comes back and says angrily, "What are you doing here, are you trying to embarrass me, go up to Klaus's room, except he isn't going to like it either, after all this isn't a nursery school."

"No, of course not," I say and leave, luckily the principal is no longer at the entrance. Since my dinner is practically ready I walk home slowly, I buy a paper at the corner newsstand, but it has the same stories as the morning paper, lots of people are out on the street, women in red and blue dresses, they crowd around the flower stand and buy sunflowers, handling them carefully, no one will live through the evening. An enormity, I think and repeat the word several times, a word of thunder and lightning, which is beginning to roar inside my head.

By now I've arrived at our building and am walking up the stairs, the children are running after me, they are hungry and in excellent spirits, the oldest has already forgotten my appearance at school. "Forget the stupid radio," he says after we've finished eating. "Why don't you help me with my homework instead, we have to write a theme for German, William Tell: Was Gessler's assassination an act of revenge or not?" "Yes," I say and look at his smooth, handsome forehead, his firm arms, "perhaps it was. I'll be right with you, I just want to hear the news for a minute." I look at my watch, it's time for the news, but there is no news, instead they are playing popular music. "So what about Tell," Arno says, "what's your opinion," and I'm thinking, Tell, the ravine, we,

CIRCE'S MOUNTAIN

too, are inside the ravine, you must flee, your time is almost up, and our time is almost up, too, only nobody knows it. No, that's not true, somebody knows, somebody has decided on popular music instead of news, somebody knows, and he sends us to our death.

"You could help me clean the aquarium," the younger of our two sons suggests. "Dad says the fish are going to suffocate, and if they suffocate, he's not going to buy me any more." The water in the aquarium is a murky brew, in which the lovely tropical fish move like gray shadows. Suffocate, I think, perhaps we will suffocate, what does the condemned man do in the last moments of his life, surely he does not write a theme for German class or wipe the slimy panes of a fishbowl. "I want to read you something," I say and go to the bookcase: Goethe's *Trilogy of Passions,* that's not for children, Jean Paul's *Hesperus,* it doesn't matter, anything, quick before they can object. Already I'm reading hurriedly yet haltingly, how can the boys understand this, but they aren't supposed to understand, only take in a few words written by a great writer, take them along into the dark we are all entering, droves of us, whole nations, shadow beside shadow, all of us faceless. I am reading, and the little one is catching the fish with a small net and putting them into a jelly jar, completely engrossed in his task. The big boy is drawing soccer players on a blotter; after a while he interrupts and says politely, "Real nice, Mom, but I don't really have time, I've got to get down to Tell." "Yes," I say and think of the line, "Square your accounts with heaven," what a thing to ask and how can you do it, square your accounts with heaven, what can you come up with except a long column of debits, and you don't have to be the tyrant Gessler for that.

"What time is it," I ask and am about to tell the children everything, but to say it, that too is an enormity, and so I wait for my husband to come home, he may know of some new developments. He arrives shortly after 5 o'clock, he brings no news, he doesn't mention my telephone call. I am standing at the window now, the cars are all going in the same direction, away from the city, not a single one is headed for downtown.

Of course, I think, but there is no point in running away; as a government employee my husband wouldn't be allowed to, no one is allowed to, no one must add to the sense of panic.

But there is no sense of panic, and I must be wrong even about the automobiles, it's so easy to imagine such things. Shortly before six, friends of ours phone and invite us over for tomorrow night, and we also have tickets for a concert. I call the box office and ask if the performance is still scheduled and a voice asks back why not. My husband has brought work home and is at his desk, the boys are playing soccer in the yard. I dig out a bunch of old photographs and take them to my husband. "Here we are," I say, "a few days after our wedding, here is our oldest at age one, here we are vacationing in Positano; look, on this one we are climbing over the rocks and here we are in the boat." Each little glued-down photo brings back a welter of memories, landscapes, conversations, quarrels and caresses, days and nights, our whole life can rise up once more, and that's what I want. I can't tell my husband that I love him, but I can show him this, a life full of love, on our last day. So I gingerly slide the first album over the files in front of my husband, and he says, "oh yes" politely and looks at a few of the old pictures. But then he looks at his watch and asks, "Can't we do this later tonight or on Sunday, I still must get some work done."

I too look at my watch; it's almost seven, curfew or Angelus bell, the sun has set, the day is over. But of course I know that it isn't over and that everything can still happen. Half an hour later my husband calls the boys in for supper, and since as usual they don't show up immediately there are angry words, including a pre-supper argument between the boys. Fathers and sons, Cain and Abel, this is how we die, with such words on our lips, with the ancient, primeval hatred.

We always have a cold meal in the evening and of course we don't pray before supper, so when I stand behind my chair and fold my hands the children are surprised and my husband looks displeased.

Nevertheless, I try, I say a little prayer that I had learned as a child and then I say all sorts of other things, red-faced and

CIRCE'S MOUNTAIN

with my words mixed-up. I give thanks for our life and ask for a merciful death. I notice that my husband wants to interrupt me and of course he does, saying firmly, "It's time to eat now," and sits down. The boys sit down, too, relieved, and ask if we'll play a card game with them after supper, specifically the quartet game with all the different makes of automobiles that I find so boring, but my husband says yes. "But let's listen to the news first," he says with a glance at me; he is probably thinking, that will calm her down, who knows what else she might start, she's having a bad day.

"Yes," I say, "we can try, but it won't work, there wasn't any news this afternoon either, nothing but popular music, including a song in Italian, *Firenze in un manto di stelle*, but no news." "Well, let's check it out," my husband says, "it's exactly 8 o'clock," and we all move into the living room, where the radio is. We sit down and wait for the eye to turn green and the familiar voice to begin talking. The eye does turn green, but there is no voice, only a sound, indescribable, a mournful, buzzing sound that grows louder and softer, like a siren and yet different, and perhaps it's not coming out of the box at all but from outside, and it's maddening. I look at my husband. He bends over the box and turns the dials, his hands are white and the veins stand out on his forehead. The children are alarmed, too, and ask, "Father, what is that? Mother, what is that?" and the little one digs his fingers into my arm.

"Who cares," I say, suddenly quite cheerful, "some silly beep, some sort of defect, let's not pay any attention. Let's play quartet. Go get the cards, and the winners get prizes tonight, first, second and third. I have a few things in my secret drawer, I'll go get them, and Klaus, could you please set the chairs in place." My husband looks at me, a terribly frightened look, but I don't want to acknowledge it, I did once, but not anymore, I've changed my mind, come around to the belief that only living can save our life. I go to the bedroom dresser, the pretty blue ball with the stars is still there, so is the flashlight, and a fire truck that's so big that I have to hide it; I wrap it in a bath towel. "Are you coming," my husband calls in a suffocating voice, yes, a suffocating voice, and I walk into the living room laughing, with my funny package under my arm. The buzzing sound is still there, but one can drown it out, we have phonograph records, we even have the song, *Firenze in un manto di stelle*, and I put that record on and set the needle down. The record is rather loud, with orchestral accompaniment, and in the meantime the oldest has dealt the cards and yells, "Who starts, me, and Daddy? In the category of trucks do you by any chance have the Goliath?" and my husband yells back, "Sorry, I don't."

Yes, this is how it will happen, and the only reason it was different in Cassandra's case is that she had no husband and children whom she had to deceive as I am now deceiving my husband and children, even though it would be logical to say, there you are, you are going to die, why didn't you believe me? But I don't say that, and at the end of this long day it has come to the point where I am deceiving myself. Nothing more will happen, I think, the day is almost gone, and I'm starting, rather noisily, to make plans, "Isn't tomorrow Sunday, no I guess not, but some Sunday soon we'll drive out to the lake. That's where we're going, do you hear?" and the kids shout, "Can we take the canoe and our swimming trunks?" and I know it's much too cold for swimming but I say yes. At this moment it will probably happen, I can't describe what, I only know we are all terrified and jump up and are hurled this way and that way, and that's how we will be found one day, I mean our skeletons, with our necks pulled in and our hands spread out. God knows what they may have held in their hands, playing cards perhaps—except that there will be no one left to find our skeletons and wonder about our family, or about any family at all.

The Fat Girl

It was late January, soon after Christmas vacation, when the fat girl came to see me. That winter I had started to lend books to the neighborhood children: they were supposed to borrow and return them on a specified day of the week. Of course I knew most of the children, but once in a while there would be strangers who did not live on our street. And while most of them stayed just long enough to exchange books, there were a few who would sit down and begin to read right then and there. I would sit at my desk and work, and the children would sit at the small table near the book wall, and their presence was a pleasure and did not distract me.

The fat girl came on a Friday or a Saturday, at least not on the day designated for the book exchange. I was planning to go out later and was just carrying a snack I had fixed into my study. I had had company, and my guest must have forgotten to close the door to the apartment. This would explain why the fat girl suddenly stood before me, just as I had put the tray down on my desk and was turning around to get something else from the kitchen. She was a girl of about twelve, wearing an old-fashioned loden coat and knitted black knee socks and carrying a pair of skates by a strap, and she seemed familiar to me, but only in a vague sort of way, and I was startled because she had appeared so silently.

"Do I know you?" I asked in surprise.

The fat girl said nothing. She only stood there and folded her hands over her round belly and looked at me with eyes as light as water.

"Did you come for a book?" I asked.

Again the girl didn't answer, but that didn't surprise me

too much. I was used to shyness on the part of the children, and that you often had to help them along. So I pulled out several books and spread them out in front of the strange girl. Then I got ready to fill out one of the cards on which I recorded the borrowed books.

"What's you name?" I asked.

"They call me Fatty," the girl said.

"Do you want me to call you that?" I asked.

"I don't care," the girl said. She did not respond to my smile, and now I seem to remember that she winced at this point. But at the time I paid no attention.

"When is your birthday?" I continued.

"In Aquarius," the girl said calmly.

Her answer amused me and I entered it on the card as a sort of joke, and then I turned back to the books.

"Are you interested in a specific book?" I asked.

But then I realized that the strange girl was not looking at the books at all, but at the tray with my tea and sandwiches.

"Perhaps you'd like to eat something," I said quickly.

The girl nodded, and her acceptance contained something like hurt surprise that I should think of this only now. She started to eat the small sandwiches, one after the other, in a peculiar manner I couldn't define until sometime later. Then she sat there again, letting her cold, listless eyes wander around the room, and there was something about her that filled me with anger and revulsion. No question about it, I hated this girl from the beginning. Everything about her repelled me, her sluggish body, her fat, pretty face, her way of talking, apathetic and arrogant at the same time. And though I had decided to give up my walk for her sake, I did not treat her with kindness, but coldly and cruelly.

Because it certainly couldn't be called kind, my sitting down at my desk with my work and saying over my shoulder, "Go on and read," when I knew perfectly well that the strange girl did not wish to read. And then I sat there intending to write, but I couldn't do it because of an odd sense of torment, similar to the torment experienced by someone who is asked to solve a riddle he can't solve, and who knows that unless he succeeds nothing will ever be the same again. And for a while I stood it, but not for long, so I turned around and started a conversation, though only the usual silly questions occurred to me.

"Do you have brothers and sisters?" I asked.

"Yes," the girl said.

"Do you like to go to school?" I asked.

"Yes," the girl said.

"What's your favorite subject?"

"Pardon?" the girl said.

"German maybe?" I asked.

"I don't know," the girl said.

I twisted the pencil between my fingers and something arose in me, a feeling of dread that was quite disproportionate to the appearance of the girl.

"Do have friends?" I asked, trembling.

"Oh yes," the girl said.

"I imagine there's one you like best?" I asked.

"I don't know," the girl said, and the way she sat there in her hairy loden coat she resembled a fat caterpillar; and she *was* like a caterpillar in the way she had eaten and the way she was now checking out her surroundings again.

That's it, nothing more to eat for you, I thought, filled with an odd desire to get even. Nevertheless I went and got bread and cold cuts, and the girl stared at them with her impassive face, and then she began to eat the way a caterpillar eats, slowly and steadily, as if driven by instinct, and I looked at her silently and with hostility.

Because by now things had come to a point where everything about this girl began to upset and annoy me. What a silly white dress, what a ridiculous stand-up collar, I thought, when the girl unbuttoned her coat after eating. I went back to my desk to work, but then I heard the girl smack her lips behind me, and this sound was like the slow plop of a black pond in the woods somewhere, and it reminded me of everything murky, everything heavy and brackish in human nature, and it irked me a great deal. What do you want with me, I thought, go away, go away. And I would have liked to take my hands and push the girl out of the room, the way one gets rid of an unwanted animal. But then I did not push her out of the room; instead I started to address her in the same unfeeling manner as before.

"Are you going to go skating now?" I asked.

"Yes," the fat girl said.

"Are you a good skater?" I asked and pointed to the skates she was still carrying.

"My sister is good," the girl said, and again there was an expression of pain and sadness on her face, and again I paid no attention.

"What does your sister look like?" I asked. "Is she like you?"

"Oh no," the fat girl said. "My sister is thin, and she has curly black hair. In summer when we're in the country and a thunderstorm comes up in the night, she gets up and sits on the railing of the highest balcony and sings."

"And you?" I asked.

"I stay in bed." the girl said. "I'm scared."

"But your sister isn't, is she?" I asked.

"No," the girl said. "She's never scared. She dives from the highest diving board. She dives in and then she swims way out . . ."

"What does your sister sing?" I asked, curious.

"She sings what she feels like singing," the girl said sadly. "She makes up poems."

"And you?" I asked.

"I don't do anything," the girl said. And then she got up and said, "I have to go now." I held out my hand, and she took it, and I don't know exactly what I felt—something like an invitation to follow her, an inaudible, urgent call. "Come back sometime," I said, but I didn't mean it, and the girl said nothing and looked at me with her cool eyes. And then she was gone and I should have felt relieved. But as soon as I heard the entrance door close, I went out into the hall and put on my coat. I ran down the stairs and reached the street just as the girl disappeared around the corner.

I've got to see this caterpillar skate, I thought. I've got to

　　　　　　　　　　　　　CIRCE'S MOUNTAIN

see how this lump of fat moves across the ice. And I walked
faster, so as not to lose track of the girl. It had been early afternoon when she arrived in my room, and now it was nearly
dusk. I had spent some years in this town as a child, but was
no longer thoroughly familiar with the layout, and though I
managed to follow the girl I soon had no idea where we were
going, and the streets and squares we passed were totally
strange to me. Also, I was suddenly conscious of a change in
the air. It had been cold, but now a thaw was setting in, and
with such a vengeance that the snow was already dripping
from the roofs and large clouds were moving across the sky.
We came to the edge of town, where the houses are surrounded by large gardens, and then there were no more
houses, and the girl suddenly disappeared down an embankment. And what I saw below me was nothing like the expected skating rink with booths and bright lights and a
glittering surface full of noise and music. What I saw was the
lake, which I had pictured as encircled by houses by now:
there it was, solitary and ringed by dark woods, looking exactly as it had when I was a child. This unexpected view affected me so much that I almost lost sight of the girl. But then
I saw her again; she was crouching at the edge of the lake, trying to cross one leg over the other and clamp the skate to her
boot with one hand while turning the key with the other. The
fat girl dropped the key a number of times, and then she
dropped down on all fours and scooted around on the ice,
searching, and she looked like an outlandish toad. In the
meantime it had been getting dark, and the landing pier for the
steamer, which jutted out into the lake a few yards from
where the girl was, lay pitch-black on the broad surface,
whose uneven silvery glint, a little darker here and there, was
an indication of the thaw. "Hurry up," I called out impatiently, and the fat girl actually did, though not because of my
urging, but because there was someone waving and shouting,
"Come on, Fatty," at the end of the long pier, someone skating in circles, a bright, buoyant figure. It occurred to me that
this must be the sister, the dancer, the stormy weather singer,
a girl after my own heart, and I was now convinced that it was

solely the wish to see this graceful creature that had brought
me here. At the same time I realized that the children were in
danger. What had started all of a sudden were the strange
groans, the deep sighs the lake seems to emit before the ice
breaks up. These sighs ran like a shuddering dirge through the
deep lake, and I heard them, but the children did not.

Surely they could not have heard them. Otherwise the fat
girl, this timid creature, would not have set out on the lake,
forging ahead with scraping, awkward movements, and her sister out there would not have been laughing and waving and
turning like a ballerina on the points of her skates, only to return to her beautiful figure eights, and the fat girl would have
avoided the dark places, which now frightened her and which
she nevertheless crossed, and her sister would not have suddenly straightened up tall and skated away, far off towards one
of the small, secluded bays.

I was able to observe all of this quite well, having started
to walk out on the pier, step by step. Though the planks were
ice-covered, I was moving faster than the fat girl below, and
when I turned around I would see the expression on her face,
impassive and filled with desire at the same time. And I could
see the cracks that were now beginning to appear everywhere,
and the foaming water that seeped through them like the foam
that seeps through the lips of a madman. And then of course I
saw the ice breaking beneath the fat girl. It happened in the
place where her sister had danced, only a few arm's lengths
from the end of the pier. I should point out right here that the
breakthrough did not threaten her life. The lake freezes in
layers, and the second layer was only three feet below and still
firm. All that happened was that the fat girl stood in three feet
of water. True, it was ice-cold and filled with crumbling floes,
but all she had to do was wade a few feet through the water to
the pier, where I could help her pull herself up. But I sus-
pected she would not make it, and for a while it looked that
way, because she just stood there scared to death, trying a few
awkward gestures while the water flooded around her and the
ice broke under her hands. Aquarius, I thought, now he will
pull you down, and I felt nothing, not the slightest sense of

CIRCE'S MOUNTAIN

pity, and did not move. But suddenly the fat girl raised her head, and because it was now quite dark and the moon had come from behind the clouds, I could see that something in her face had changed. Her features were the same and yet not the same; they were broken open by passion and determination, as if now, in the face of death, they were drinking in life, all the life that was burning in the world. I was convinced she was about to die and that this was final, so I bent over the railing and looked down at the white face, which looked back at me like my own reflection. But then the fat girl reached the post. She reached out and started to pull herself up, holding on rather skillfully to the nails and hooks that projected from the wood. Her body was too heavy, her fingers were bleeding, and she kept falling back, but only to try again. I was watching a long struggle, a terrible wrestling for liberation and transformation, like the breaking apart of a shell or cocoon, and now I wanted to help the girl, but I also knew that my help had become unnecessary, because now I knew who she was.

I don't remember walking home that night. I only remember on the stairs I told a neighbor that there was still a piece of lakeshore with green banks and black woods, but she replied that I was mistaken. And that the papers on my desk were all mixed up, and somewhere in that jumble I came across an old snapshot of myself in a white wool dress with a stand-up collar, with light, watery eyes, very fat.

Circe's Mountain

Friday

Here, under the fig tree, one could begin to live again; to live, meaning different things for different people and meaning, for me, to love and to write. Except I don't mean the act of writing itself, which is torture, but the special looking and listening that leads to it. Here, under the fig tree, one morning after a breakfast of pitch black espresso, tiny eggs and bread without butter. After Felice has stopped his three-wheeler and called from behind the hedge, *"Oggi tutto a posto?"*—a polite way of offering a sales pitch, since of course he is hoping that we will respond with fervent no's and rush out to fill our baskets with tomatoes and beans and hard, green peaches. After the garbage truck drives by, raising tremendous dust, and we have forgotten as usual to set out the can and have to run after the truck, wrapped in a dust cloud, and the men have already stopped and are walking back towards us, laughing goodnaturedly. In the morning, when the irresistible Mauro comes around the corner and parks his Vespa in the shade at Pozzo's, sometimes with a friendly hello and sometimes without a word, and you can read in his face what happened on the dance floor the night before, whether Costanza was nice to him or ignored him or, worse, drove off with the engineer to the beautiful, spooky mountainside hotel or to the moonlit Temple of Jupiter—he knows what goes on there. And last night Costanza and Annamaria really did go up there, but at the crucial moment Costanza did her inimitable number: the whiny voice and, what does he mean, *bella luna,* there's not a star or a fishing boat to be seen and it's a cold night; she feels chilled. So they drove back, and twice there was a black cat by the side of the road, and each time the engineers, these two grown men, stopped and shifted into reverse and backed to the nearest crossing, so that they drove home on bad and chancy roads, all in order to avoid passing the cat. The girls are telling me about this, one lying in the hammock, the other in the lawn chair; they stretch, reluctant to start in on the day's tasks of practicing the flute and learning vocabulary, and their voices are like breakers that come and go and try to pull me with them back into life. And my night was long and wakeful, a restless turning over on my rustling straw sack, a mental walk along the beach, along the seam of the waves, where the sand is damp and hard, past the stands of reeds and the cave entrances, always looking for a body, the tall, slender body of a youth, your body washed up by the sea, washed up by death because the sea is death. I wanted to embrace and awaken your body, or perhaps not awaken, only embrace it, because disintegrating in the ground, becoming bone, is worst of all—what have we to do with bones. "Didn't you sleep well?" Annamaria asks and Costanza says, "It's the moon's fault; the ocean moon is dangerous," and then she jumps up and scolds the dirty-white hen we call Candida, which struts past us every morning into the dining room, where it deposits something black and damp. Annamaria sighs and clears away the dishes, and Costanza goes to the bedroom, from where we soon hear the first sounds of her flute, monotonous, harsh, unpleasant, warming-up sounds.

Saturday
It begins with the eyes, which had stopped seeing anything, colors, shapes, only a gray mishmash, and which did not wish to see anything either, since your eyes lie broken and collapsed. Because every act of looking and perceiving is an act of survival, and survival is betrayal. And please don't remind me of the fairy tale about the pitcher of tears, about the dead child who pretends to suffer when its mother's tears fill the pitcher to overflowing; that tale is simply the invention of survivors who are greedy for life, people who are sick of weeping and who don't want to imagine how lonely the dead

CIRCE'S MOUNTAIN

are, how terribly alone. But for those who do imagine it, black, all-consuming moss covers the retina and their ears are so stopped up that they can't hear life's siren song, which is not necessarily lovely and musical, but may only be the cries of a donkey in a field of artichokes or the barking of dogs in the night. Even so, one day it begins: the eyes see again, for instance here in San Felice, the image of Circe in the rock-cliff, her stony head thrown back, facing the merciless sun. A great profile in the southern sky, Circe turned to stone, like Niobe, like all the truly despairing; Circe the magician, whose prodigious arts could not hold Odysseus and were powerless against his homesickness for Ithaca, for death. It was Circe's head that caught my eye today, naked, terrible and beautiful above the cork oak forests of Torre Paola, and it didn't matter that some lively friends from Rome who visited us later in the day transferred the legend to the Black Sea: Circe, Odysseus, the transformed sailors all moved to the Hellespont. My eyes were suddenly open anyway; gone was the black moss over the retina, gone the thought of betrayal, and my tears sufficed only to cover the delicate colors of the adventurous sea with a glaze of mother-of-pearl.

Sunday

No question, voluntarily or not, I am on the road back (back from where? from inertia, paralysis, being stone), on a road that is like the underground passage between Lake Avernus and Cumae, whose darkness is pierced occasionally by light falling through holes in the vaulted ceiling. Light, causing us to look up at laurel and lemons and fruit-bearing orange branches, a vista of life and paradise for the northerner, who tends to feel too much at home between the lake of the underworld and the sibyl's grotto. The road back to reality, except that where we are living this summer there are neither laurel nor lemon trees nor fruit-bearing orange trees. Because we live in the plateau from which the rock juts as starkly as the fist of the man who was buried alive, who was found one night by our neighbor (a full moon night, of course) and whom I'll tell about later. A fist, a hand, a fan, and on the mountainside the flora of the southern islands, the natural one of *macchia* and olive groves and the cultivated one of roses, geraniums and shrill bougainvilleas, with scrub oak in the gorges and, in the shadow of the cliff wall, orange trees and grapes. But as I said, except for the fist, the fan, there's nothing like Klingsor's enchanted garden; the rest is flat terrain, roads white with dust, herb gardens crusted with salt and dust, artichoke and grain fields. Barley is being harvested right now, not with threshers, not even scythes, but with sickles, those moon-round, short-handled knives, as in ancient times. Men with sickles suddenly pop up from their bent positions, burning eyes in deeply tanned, sweaty faces, and ask the girls for the time, follow them, and Costanza and Annamaria hurry away frightened, calling back over their shoulders many times, "L'una e mezza." Reed and cane and the local tree, the eucalyptus, cool and slender, with silvery, slightly wavy leaves that hang close to the trunk and heap around it on the ground in shades of flesh and lilac, decaying gracefully, without pathos, without stiffening and flaming anger. That's what it looks like around here, around our cottage and beyond, and the public beach between here and Terracina is a dirty wasteland, strewn with garbage. Sometimes a few boys are there towards evening, playing soccer between the water and the wall of reeds, and the little horse pulls a cart full of iron poles along the edge of the water. The black, sluggish canals from the interior bring a swampy smell, a smell of melancholy and autumn, into the salty freshness. What else shall I tell you, silent heart, and do you want to hear it, do you want to hear anything at all?

Monday

Eyes, new eyes for Costanza, for her calm, sure gestures, for her inexpressibly pure, lucid gaze. As though I had returned from a long trip and suddenly find she has reached her majority; my darkness was for her a beneficial shade, my dullness a *ritardando* that adjusted our steps to a side-by-side movement, so that I no longer run ahead and pull her behind me as I did when she was little. The fear, the everlasting burning, parental fear of having neglected something, of having left something important unsaid, has diminished. Knowing that she is all I have now, I also know that I no longer have her, cannot demand anything from her, not even understanding for my crippled state, my self-hatred. I have to hide the fact that I belong to you, a dead man, and therefore to death. I must stop telling her about our love, this singular union between two people, which must ultimately strike her as grotesque and inhuman. Because the wheel has already turned once: autumn, winter, spring, summer; it has been a long time and a daughter, of all people, must set herself free. Each generation has its own way of living and loving, or of not loving, or of waiting, and one day a mother is jolted back to the recognition that this counts, too, this slow, irrevocable easing back into life and finding a home in music, the least human of the arts. One day she cannot help listening to the flute passages and realizing that every child is a stranger and yet so dear and familiar in her fears and dangers, her love of life and longing for death. That, and all the things that come into play in Costanza's case: the demonic waters of the Danube and your ride on horseback across Poland in a tattered uniform; my paths through the vineyards and beechwoods of the Breisgau; and the last Schnaewelin, the dwarf.

Tuesday

The often-mentioned moon, that disturber of sleep and kindler of love, is rising over the ocean, a round opening in the sky's shifting umbrella, a hole backlit by a gentle fire. Only later does it grow large and silver, casts its light on the water and then disappears on the other side of the mountain, so that it is already behind us and only the fishermen out there can see its trembling light on the waves.

Sitting on the terrace at Cartuzza's, with my feet on the balustrade, I look at it sleepily, unable to comprehend that it is to be ignited, that the cool Selene is to become a vehicle for the fortunes of our planet's wars. They talk about that in the small lobby of the hotel; they show and tell. There sit the children, up too late, tiny in the large chairs, staring at the screen, and on the screen there are children, clusters of children with their mothers, children of men who will soon be encased in a capsule and shot up to the moon. "Well, well," the nice TV men say, "aren't you glad that your daddy, of all people," and the children, clutching their toys, say they are so happy they can't wait. And the well-coiffed mothers are equally happy; each one hopes her husband will be first. Stand by, ladies and gentlemen—and the whole world holds its breath. The wives and children of heroes, while out there the cool Selene has risen higher, filling up the woods and valleys, including the woods and valleys of the Black Forest, and while I stare at her, the disc of the dance floor, round and silvery, rises towards her, rises with all its dancing couples above the white-blooming oleander, the heads of the mimosa and pepper trees and the thatched roof of the bar hut, and a sad melody follows the transported dancers and exhorts a young murderer, *hang down your head and cry*, and then it stops and the light goes out. The wind springs up, iron poles clang, and sand blows across the terrace.

Wednesday

Ears, new ears for the stories that circulate here; for example, the story about the man who was buried alive, which was told to me in explicit detail this morning by my hairdresser. My hairdresser knows all about it because the hero, i.e., the dead man who suddenly raised his fist, was his cousin. And of course he also knew the other characters, the pale, beautiful Nanna, who became the cousin's lover and lived with him and raised flowers in tin cans on his terrace, all of them in knock-out red—fuchsias, geraniums and salvias—and who wore a necklace of black wooden beads. "Ehi, Nanna," the cousin would call from afar, evenings when he came home from his work as a mason, gunning his motorcycle, and Nanna's pale face would peer out from among the flowers while young Gianni disappeared down the stairs and out the back door. The cousin noticed nothing; and isn't someone who notices nothing worse than someone who looks out and takes action; isn't he disgusting in his smug certainty and pride of owner-

CIRCE'S MOUNTAIN

ship; doesn't he virtually beg for disaster and bloodletting; doesn't he himself really plunge the knife into his guts? Young Gianni spends the late afternoons with Nanna; in the evening he is cast out and goes to the movies, where he studies knifings, throttlings and shots from the hip, all possible methods of silencing a man who doesn't talk much anyway. That he loved his rival, perhaps more than he loved the girl, is an observation that engages the hairdresser so much that he leaves off working on my hair, lights a cigarette and blows the smoke towards the dim mirror. "Maybe that's why he did it halfheartedly," I say and think about this southern love of men, of women, this world embrace, and the hairdresser throws the cigarette into the washbasin and tells me the facts: how Gianni and Nanna put the dead cousin on his motorcycle, tying his arms around Gianni's chest, and Nanna got on behind with a shovel across her knees. Because they had to hide the body, bury it, but most of all hide it, and it would do no good to throw it into the sea; the sea won't keep anyone, it washes off the blood but doesn't close the wounds. So they buried him, a quick, bungled job, in a rain-soaked piece of ground far from the vineyards of the village, in the valley near the tourist cottages. Buried him, but not deeply, as if, once the job had been done, they didn't really care—shallowly enough for him to have come to the surface, but surely it didn't occur to them that he would initiate his own surfacing. "Time for the dryer," I say at this point in the hairdresser's story and reach for it myself, to put the humming shell over my head, because the story is starting to get to me; black fists are sprouting in my neighbors' gardens among the Roman camomiles. And the cousin was beyond help; everyone is beyond help; you, me; as fate would have us.

Thursday

To write, describe, create a miniature world—and then the question why; why do I begin again. Because I can't live in shapeless darkness, or because I want to remind you of what was so dear to you here: above all the landscape that you loved as the stage of human desire and restlessness, but also as creation, as stone and wall and herb. Having the advantage of the overview may make one homesick for what's small and near, just as the air traveler, beneath whose feet the puzzling mosaic of the earth's surface is pulled along, yearns suddenly for the mouldy smell of harbors, wants to crumble rain-soaked dirt in his hand, rest his forehead against prickly grass. Since I can no longer give you anything else, I will give you this: Ristorante Cartuzza, a bar in a straw hut, a juke box, bushes and trees and faded canvas umbrellas—all this toy-size in my hand and newly erected for you between the road and the sea. Not to forget the little chairs, reddish-white wooden chairs that I set up, tiny, but doesn't everything have to be tiny for your eyes now, toys for the giant; and the farmer with his plow, the horses, the girl giant and the scolding giant father, all are dead.* Toys for a giant, this summer beach, this small life of two months, and the special game: the glass-covered case in which a ball rolls down the slanting surface between bright, bell-ringing obstacles and lights that flash on without warning, the ball intent on hiding in a black hole. But there's the lever that can flip up two barriers at just the right moment, and the ball returns to the labyrinth, the little columns and flashing lights, no rest, not for a long time yet, and a board on top of the case is registering numbers—points earned? lifespans? Not to forget the glass automat that swallows coins and propels small records forward until they drop down, *When you smile at me, Giulia,* and *Catch a falling star,* but we're in June, too early for meteor showers. Not to forget the flagpole on Cartuzza's terrace and the blinking light that the young waiters—children in long pants and white jackets—use as playful signals in the evening when the excursion boat returns from Ponza. Short short, long long, and from faraway, out of the white twilight, engulfing sea and sky together, comes the blinking reply.

---

*The references here are to a popular German children's story.

CIRCE'S MOUNTAIN

Friday

In the morning, everything on the beach seems clear and orderly and yet it isn't, not even the activities of the children, who are so pleasantly busy with their little spades and buckets. If you look at them with the sensitive and perpetually astonished eyes of someone who has long been blind, they become part of the masque of human passions, which they perform with grace and mystery. Beach games, sand games, which make very little use of the big ocean, even though it's shallow a long way out, as Annamaria proved on our first evening when, pursued by the eyes of all the young men, she took off her sandals and lifted her skirt and slip above her hips to wade under stars through the black water and catch the dinghy of a motorboat—a contessa's prank, an act of childish willfulness, which encouraged the notion that my daughters are crazy. But they are not my present subject; my subject is little Nina with the chubby, red face and singleminded routine. She fetches a bucket of water while holding a large comb in her left hand; then she puts down the bucket and switches the comb to her right and begins to comb everyone's hair, her mother's, her father's, her big brothers', her aunts', her girlfriends', sometimes dipping the comb into the water and occasionally fetching more water. Finally the whole family protests, but the people under the next beach umbrella are willing. All morning she does nothing except comb and smooth (again, again!), with her fat little hands and her red, serious face. And Peppino is my subject too, Peppino who insists on burying his mother in the sand. Cover the legs, pat the sand down (the toes, those intractable little animals), cover the arms, cover stomach and chest—it keeps rising and falling and making cracks in the sand; cover the neck and the hair until nothing is left except a small, spooky triangle with rolling eyes and snapping lips, and Peppino is scared and about to run away, but his mother breaks through the crust laughing, and Peppino begs *again* and screams and stomps his feet until she lets him. Also there's Joan, a six-year-old from England with a wild, rough voice and explosive gestures, who is hiding under a beach towel, and the adults know perfectly what is required of them: "I wonder where Joan is," followed by lengthy speculations—on top of an elephant in Africa, on an ice floe at the North Pole, and for a long time Joan doesn't move until finally she is overcome by homesickness and pulls the beach towel off her head, but sometimes she gets caught in it and can't breathe and rolls around in a circle, a red and blue bundle. "Here's Joan," she cries at the end, triumphant and consoling, and exposes her pink face, which is surrounded by damp ringlets, and already she reaches (again, again) for the same magic cloak of invisibility so that the game can start over. And oh yes, the little boys who jump off the bright terrace down to the beach at night, a jump of three meters down to the moonlit, naked sand where the umbrella stands rise like tree stumps left in a war zone, a landscape so foreign that they throw down their red sandals first, needing something familiar to receive them. But as soon as they've landed they slip into their sandals and run towards the stairs to stand up there again and feel the shiver of fear, unclench their hands again from the balustrade and jump, again, again . . .

Saturday

Each day I see the world more clearly. Shadows become figures, white splotches become faces, dark holes become eyes with wants and troubles. People you don't know and whom I hate for that reason, but I must be aware of them and put them into the margins of my life story—something I had hoped would never exist, only our common story, and then the ending. But here it is, a sad and timid story, and here are people with whom I shake hands and whose health I inquire about, and they inquire about mine and look at me shyly. For example, there are the young men on the beach, Mauro the moody one, and Mago and the engineer, two young men who share a room together and work together on a construction project that makes the shore road unusable just when the summer people are here; there's a deep ditch, a high dirt wall, and a fire-engine red machine that swings its phantom arms up and down. The friends spend their evenings at Cartuzza's, where they talk, that is, the engineer does the talking; after six years at the university he knows how to put words together, but who would have paid for the higher education of Giulio, called Mago the rainmaker; he had to go to work as soon as he finished school. So he just sits there, gazing fixedly at Costanza, distracted only when the boys jump off the terrace, which upsets him but doesn't interest the engineer, who pays no attention. "Quit doing that," Mago pleads, "you could land on a piece of glass or a rusty nail," but no one listens to him; the boys jump and the engineer goes on talking, say about the grotto they uncovered (though only their boss's name got in the paper), or about the sea monster with the giant foot and large and small heads; junk, an ill-assorted piece of rock, first interpreted as the snake-encircled Laocoon but now said to be Polyphemus or the sea monster Scylla. It is getting late, the music is playing and the engineer, spoiled as he is, jumps up and simply extends his hand towards Annamaria, while Mago leans across the table towards Costanza and asks, "Would you like to dance?" and he smiles the indescribably sad smile of southern Italian boys who are beautiful and poor and hopelessly lonely.

Sunday

Some people carry their rightful chair or bed around with them, the way the snail carries its home, except invisibly. Only when they actually materialize do we recognize the appropriateness of these objects and smile with relief. Yes, we think, that suits you, the office chair, the saddle, the wide bed, the coffin. The hammock was invented for Annamaria—but where can you still find hammocks these days? When we were children we lugged heavy hammocks to the fir forest and stretched them across the narrow stream that hurried downhill among moss-covered stones. Meant for reading, sleeping and especially daydreaming, they seemed to belong to those long-gone childhood days, destined to die with them. So I am surprised that we have a hammock here, though it's a different kind of hammock; made of thin nylon, it can be tucked into a tiny bag and needs no wooden hangers; it envelops the body like a fisherman's net, like a cocoon. The owner, who has lent it to Annamaria, never uses it; he is a modern, i. e., restless and busy man for whom a day, even a few hours of leisure is too much. But here the hammock is a prized item; it elicits admiration, and in the absence of sumptuous meals for our guests we offer it to them right after their arrival. They sit in it sideways, letting their feet hang over, making the hammock swing by pushing off against the terrace tiles. Sometimes Costanza lies in it, with her work in her lap. But only Annamaria is born for it; she alone carries it around invisibly, as the snail does its home. She alone still knows how to dream those old girlhood dreams, he and I, I and he, dreams that require that the he have more than one face, figure, set of gestures. His faces smile at the old-fashioned girl through the branches of the fig tree, and when she sways back and forth, casting tender glances upwards, she no doubt hears voices, many voices that all tell her the same thing, and that is the best part, since of course girls in hammocks are afraid of the reality of love and imagine it to be horrible. Their attitude towards life hangs in the balance; don't grab for it, not yet, don't choose any of the countless possibilities the future offers because you will close the door on all others. Just sway back and forth in the net, the cocoon, and smile at someone, at no one, with a tender look. That's Annamaria, who is actually not my daughter at all but is thought of as my daughter here. To describe her, one comes up with old-fashioned words: willful, sprightly, roguish, and she herself has constructed a child's world out of miniatures: little house, little tree, little hen. Relieving an old woman of her bundle of wood comes as naturally to her as the sudden attacks of sadness and helplessness which bring an expression of fear to her rosy-cheeked face.

Monday

Already I want to pull back from my new interest in people and things, don't want my imagination to stir, don't want to invent, much less feel pleasure. I don't want to abandon you in your loneliness, your powerlessness, your muteness, which I cannot share. Instead of walking home from the beach with Costanza and Annamaria, who laugh and chatter the whole way, I leave by myself under the pretext of picking up groceries or starting lunch. I take a completely different road; it's hotter, brighter and much longer. Even though I've tied a black kerchief underneath my wide straw hat the sun beats down mercilessly. There's no one about; I meet no one and am overtaken by no one. The shuttered houses are like empty sea shells; a grille is pulled across the door of the general store. My feet grind through the dust; gravel gets into my sandals and I have to shake my feet to lighten the load. At a certain bend in the road a strong, sweet, citrusy scent wafts across a garden fence; I stop there for a moment and also by the ragged field of dried-up artichoke plants, above whose wild, iron spikes a few delicate blue flowers float as if they had dropped from the sky. Sometimes I meet the men whose job is insect control and they appeal to me in their non-humanness, with their elephant masks, their long-handled, white-spouted canisters, their coats dusted with greenish-blue powder. What appeals to me, too, is that at this hour no one talks, no one sings or turns on the radio, and that the only sound I hear is the insistent, irritating but totally inorganic chirping of countless cicadas. On this road I hardly think at all, not even of you. But I feel good being seen by no one and therefore being no one, because no one sees you anymore and you are no one. My evenings alone (I walk the girls over to Cartuzza's because that's the custom here, *la mamma*, have a drink and go back home)—the evenings are different, less inorganic, sadder, plagued by memories, disturbed by visions.

Tuesday

By the light, which falls on the terrace through the living room door, I am reading letters from the Great Beyond in a French book. A woman whose son died at the age of fifteen spent years recording daily communications from him. The young angel is as severe as a young son: he judges his mother as too worldly, too distracted; he often finds her unwilling to be absorbed in him, or even to encounter him. He is able to be in touch with her because he was so young and innocent when he died; he does not have to endure the purgatorial

Circe's Mountain   121 fires, only an undefined, drifting existence in the Beyond, and he has so far been denied the vision of the Mother of God. Mutual faith is the medium through which his voice is carried; the obligatory hocus-pocus, the rapping and dancing lights, don't count. The son is preparing his mother for Heaven, lovingly and impatiently. She is to loosen her hold on the earth, become a spirit like himself, which is possible in the paradisal landscape of the Church. However, there is nothing in her account that points to an increase in spirituality and a lessening of the worldliness, which would lead, in the end, to a transcendent death. Nothing like that, but no defection either, no liberation from this superhuman discipline. The book is finished; no doubt the dictation continues night after night and even during the day, an act of will unlike any other, fidelity beyond the grave regardless of whether the speaker is really her dead son or her own profuse imagination giving voice to a shadow. I think there is a reason, besides the theological one, why only a boy who is practically still a child can appear in this manner or be called forth in this manner by his survivors. We don't want to think of our older dead, least of all you, as so grimly humorless; on the contrary, we imagine that at the moment of passing over they become truly wise and lenient vis-à-vis the childish games still played out by the survivors. No, in this respect I would not be afraid to get in touch with you. That isn't the reason I don't pick up pencil and paper when I sit on the terrace alone at night, my thoughts wholly on you. I could endure everything except that I might hear nothing, have nothing to write down, that the page might be darkened only by the moving shadows of the fig leaves, gone by morning.

Wednesday

My old curiosity has come back. For the first time since we have arrived here I have climbed up to the town, a mountain town whose narrow streets and piazzas thunder like machine shops from the rumbling of engines. The appealing order of black and white squares in the pavement is covered with plenty of disorder, all sorts of garbage and rivulets of dirty water. Here and there a stairway with a curved wrought iron banister leads up to a house, and roses and carnations can be seen blooming in tin cans behind scrolled balcony railings. Girls carry water home from the well in rounded jugs decorated with Mycenaean molluscs. On the stone walls of the houses there are black-bordered pieces of paper, which mourn the death of an inhabitant, and the stone bench by the town gate is occupied by the old, old as stone. Anyone entering or leaving the town has to pass them; they are like markers reminding him that youth cannot last. The Templars are still present in the names of the streets and inns, but the memory of the inhabitants is short, and the only past owner of the castle they can name is someone who bought it two generations ago for a song. Who really rules this place, and probably always has, is the ancient woman with the bony fingers and the ring of flies around her lips. She sits on the stone bench in front of her tiny house, emaciated, skeletal, with the glowing eyes of a cat. An enormous hairy spider hangs above her head on the crudely plastered wall behind her. Through the half-open curtain one can see her windowless hovel, a bed heaped with gray rags and a stove beneath bunches of dried herbs. There is no way of talking to the old woman. Not that she's deaf or mute, but she is completely indifferent, or interested only in a story hidden from the rest of us, which has gone on for thousands of years. And since I've come across her not just here in the country but in the cities, within a hundred yards of their marble facades; since she exists not once but countless times, I am familiar with her and recognize her other faces as well, some of them frightening, as if she were capable of wandering around in the night, choking little children to death. I have a sense of her toughness, the toughness of ants that cannot be wiped out by even the heaviest foot. I also have a sense of her crushing power, her complicity with sickness, hopelessness, despair. There are moves afoot to expel her and it has happened that her ramshackle dwelling has been torn down behind her back. Then she has risen without a word, moved on and settled down elsewhere, in front of a quonset hut, a cave in the mountainside or a suburban slum whose gorges admit no light. And she sits there, as I saw her today in the mountain town, with a ring of flies around her bluish lips and an old triumph in her splintered eyes. And the spider above her head has finished its net and waits in the heat of the noon hour, a black spot on a blindingly white wall.

Thursday

Wandering around alone, that is to say, with you, except without talk, without response, without touch, without glances of agreement—wandering around on Circe's mountain, which sits on top of flat tidal land. This rock belongs to the Mediterranean islands, not to the coast; the people living up there are essentially islanders and it is easy to imagine every possible act of island violence occurring in this isolation, summary justice, blood revenge, frontier law. Today I saw several men standing in a grape arbor and pointing to another man, dressed in city clothes, who had evidently arrived by bus and was now walking up the steep road. Not a stranger but one of them, and yet they seemed to have something against him and to be plotting to play a trick on him or possibly something worse. The man didn't notice them; like someone returning after a long absence, he looked ahead at the houses crowded together below the summit and with his head thrown back, his happy smile seemed to fix on one particular house. I felt like warning him, but that was only because of a story I had heard and which took place elsewhere, on a real island; what happened here had nothing to do with that and might be quite harmless. In the story nothing was harmless. The returning man was a Cypriot who had collaborated with the British and who had remained with them after the cessation of hostilities, thus enjoying their protection from his own countrymen. He spent many months in a military barracks surrounded by barbed wire, was well fed and treated humanely. But as time went on he became more and more homesick for his mountain village, so much so that he became physically ill, and finally he asked to be allowed to go home. The British sent a police escort along, who accompanied him as far as the entrance to his village and then gladly left him to himself. In the

CIRCE'S MOUNTAIN

meantime the returnee had been spotted coming up the mountain and the news of his arrival had spread. The townspeople had assembled in front of his house as if to welcome him, but what took place was not a celebration but an execution. The man's wife, sensing danger, had started to run ahead and warn him, but they tied her to the bedpost, leaving the door open. She was to witness what would happen to her husband; a traitor's wife was guilty too. She hung there, screaming and crying, as she watched relatives and old friends lug gasoline cans and straw. They intended to dowse the homesick traitor with gasoline and let him burn like a torch, and that's exactly what they did, and the man was too surprised to protest, or perhaps he expected nothing else, but felt compelled to go home anyway. This scene was on my mind today when I stood next to the grape arbor and listened for sounds from the place above where the man and the men in the arbor had gone by different routes. But what I heard was nothing horrendous, no screams, only the cheerful sounds of a brass band playing a friendly welcome.

Friday

To ride in a motorboat that rises halfway out of the water and performs the most darings leaps and turns at high speed— one must feel supernatural doing that, I thought as I was sitting on the rim, my face covered with spray, salt and wind. Today, when I was invited for a ride, I did feel the sense of freedom which strikes one as divine, but at the same time my body was bothered by the repeated vehement jolts inflicted on the body by the boat hitting the water. The noise of the motor was thunderous and my view of the beach changed constantly: now white sand and colorful beach umbrellas, now the ragged line of cliffs, and already we were heading south towards Terracina and the Temple of Jupiter. Speed transformed the boat into a mythical bird, but the rough bumps made it seem more like a wild horse whose rider can barely stay on top, his head reeling under its bucking. But then the motor stalled and we glided soundlessly over the water and it all came back, a clear head, forests of algae, fish, and Vineta way down below the ocean's mirror, raising its shadowy towers and ringing its mysterious bells. I remembered us, on a beach much farther south, coming home from a boat trip in the evening and bending over the water: there were real ruins there, the remains of a gradually engulfed town, but I thought even then what was really down there was the great landscape of the dead, not just the drowned, and that in the end everything that lived, loved and suffered on earth descends there. And all memory, too, so that the same places can exist on land and below, only below they embody their past, time that cannot be lived again. Down there is where the real Rome, Athens and Istanbul lie for me, cities I shared with you, and there is nothing funereal about them. In fact, today I thought all I had to do was slip down and I would be surrounded again by the electric life that they once had for you and me. While the boat was still gliding along soundlessly, I thought of Vineta as a great bazaar of memories, conversations that sound again and forgotten faces that look out of windows. I paid no attention to the owner of the boat, who was busying himself with the motor and swearing; I only heard the voice of my young companion cheerfully offering to pick a bouquet of algae, *for you, Madame*, as he started to reach into the water. But the sudden loud roar of the motor catapulted us forward again; the beach raced past, the cliffs and the lighthouse, and the sea congealed into a hard, glassy surface on which we performed our unruly dance until everything, the hot sun, the flying spray and the naked azure sky raised the relentless cry of *today, today* once more.

Saturday

To move away and come back, to leave people and the world and then approach them again, this is motion not subject to a pendulum. Long and short periods of darkness, long and short periods of light.

The darkness of isolation requires that we bring its knowledge back with us; one can't simply start in where one left off. And this is even more true after a sojourn to the edge of the bearable, a half-death. We assume that new words will offer

126

themselves to the writer, new colors to the painter, that newly apparent connections will occur to the thinker. Disappointingly, this is not the case. Even after the most excruciating experience we obey the law of gravity; our legs go down and our heads up; we wake up, put on our clothes and go out, remaining in the skin we wanted to jump out of, at least in spirit. We have become sadder and probably less curious but not new, and the pool of words to express the incredible is no greater than it was. Nor is the intonation different, not without some wrenching spasm to change it, because it belongs not only to the individual but to a whole generation. Even intense, heartbreaking experience does not enable us to discover the language of tomorrow; even the sounds of today's speech are already unusable for the older writer who still reserves a place for physical reality, sense perception, and for whom the sign has not entirely replaced the image. Not to go on as before, this is the wish of everyone who has not chosen his new beginning but has had it imposed on him, with no inkling of how and where it will lead him. We want to get off the old track, find new escape routes, reappear with a new voice and face. Instead we find we are the same person, with little more to say than before, and we have not discovered new forms. In fact, we may feel at times that the years spent in darkness have magically multiplied, so that we cannot understand current speech and the importance of things other people consider important. What is left of us, other than silence, is monologue, monologue born of struggle and discipline, which may still have some meaning just because of this struggle and discipline. An accounting to the self in the old, no longer welcome way, with a heavier heart.

Sunday

To go on writing, go on living, with a heavier heart than before. Suitcases packed; our last Circeo night behind us; last dance music borne across the dark beach, *Catch a falling star, Hang down your head and cry*; ball that runs the ringing obstacle course to its dark shelter and is whipped back; magically switched-on numbers—who holds on longest wins. I don't

want to hold on, don't want to be bumped back and forth between the gaudy lights, and yet something has pulled me back
into life and forced my eyes open: *you are not ready for the
hole, pull yourself together, what you make of it is up to you.*
Each day I have seen and heard and thought a little more and
have not given up my dead love; he has been in my mind always. So much so that I am fearful he might stay behind here
when I get on the bus, San Felice-Roma, in front of the Neanderthal Hotel, where they keep that prehistoric skull in a cave.
They'll all be there waving: the dissimilar young men and the
dissimilar sisters, the hairdresser, and the photographer with the
funny little African cap, who took two pictures of Costanza, one
as a flower among flowers in a garden and the other in her bathing suit, with a frightened question in her eyes, but that was not
his intention. The same old music from Majolatis's beach terrace, always the same tunes and voices; it is only July, the summer season still running its merry-go-round, the autumn storms,
early nights and desolation of September still ahead. Our cottage
has been rented again; as I write this the new family is arriving
on the terrace and Annamaria wants to put the little darkhaired
boys in the hammock before she takes it down and folds it up,
but the children are afraid; they've never seen anything like
that. Hard to part from the fig tree, its fruits now ripe and dry,
almost inedible; it was my companion on the terrace at night, an
enchanted human being who sometimes sighed and waved his
arms. But it was not you. You are not spellbound into one
shape, and I am homeless and restless because I don't know
where to look for you. My one fear is that you might be left behind here. Already I picture us driving away: the road winds
around twice and runs along the back of the mountain: Circe's
head, thrown back and turned to stone; the grounds of the Roman villa, which, though sub-divided into lots, are still a wilderness; and as we are driving away perhaps your airy steps are
already proceeding towards the home of the enchantress, towards the black bushes from which Odysseus saw mysterious
smoke issuing and from which lions and wolves leapt into view.

128   CIRCE'S MOUNTAIN

Marie Luise Kaschnitz was one of Germany's most esteemed writers, an important spiritual and intellectual force, particularly for the work published after World War II. She was the winner of every major literary prize her country gave, including the Goethe Prize, the Immermann Prize, the Hebel Prize, and the Büchner Prize, as well as being the recipient of several honorary doctorates. Kaschnitz lived in Italy much of her life; as a result, both Germany and southern Italy serve as locales for her work. She was as acclaimed for her books of poetry as for her prose, which included fiction and highly innovative nonfiction, as well as radio plays and a biography.

Kaschnitz's novels, novellas and collections of stories include *Liebe beginnt; Elissa; Das dicke Kind; Das Haus der Kindheit; Lange Schatten; Ferngespräche,* and *Vogel Rock.* She also wrote acclaimed imaginative prose works such as *Engelsbrücke; Wohin denn ich; Tage, Tage, Jahre; Orte* and *Beschreibung eines Dorfes.*

Lisel Mueller's titles include *The Need to Hold Still* (winner of the 1981 National Book Award), *The Private Life* (the 1975 Lamont Poetry Selection), *Second Language*, and *Dependencies*. Her fifth major collection of poems, *Waving From Shore*, was recently published by Louisiana State University Press.

She is the translator of the *Selected Later Poems of Marie Luise Kaschnitz* (Princeton University Press) and *Whether Or Not* (Juniper Press), a collection of prose poems by Kaschnitz. She has also translated a verse play by Hugo von Hofmannsthal, and the novel *Three Daughters* (Harcourt Brace) by W. Anna Mittgutsch.

CIRCE'S MOUNTAIN

The text is Garamond ITC
set by Stanton Publication Services and
printed by Thomson-Shore Inc.
on Glatfelter acid-free paper.
Design and Graphics by
R.W. Scholes.

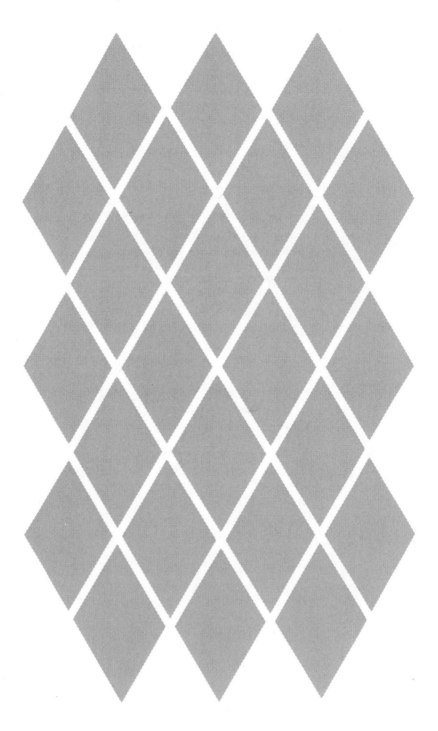